"How dare you do this to me again?"
Pellea demanded.

"This isn't like before," he protested.

"Here you are, sneaking into my country, just like before. Here you are, hiding in my chambers again. Just like before."

"But this time, when I leave, you're going with me."

She stared at him, hating him and loving him at the same time.

For just a split second, she allowed herself to give in to her emotions. How she would love to throw herself into his arms and hold him tight, to feel his hard face against hers, to sense his heart pound as his interest quickened.

But she couldn't do that. She'd spent too many nights dreaming of him, dreaming of his tender touch. She had to forget all that. Too many lives depended on her.

Dear Reader,

For the island nation of Ambria, the time of reckoning is fast approaching. The storm is gathering. Retribution for what was done to the DeAngelis royalty when their country was torn from them is at hand, and Pellea Marallis, promised to the usurper's heir, knows this very well.

Monte DeAngelis, the crown prince, has come back to claim what is his. For most of his life he's known exactly what that is. Only now does he see that his need has grown. Though he never thought he would let a woman blur the intensity of his determination, Pellea is doing just that. In the grand scheme of things, he is afraid he may just ache for her more strongly than he craves revenge.

The more he tries to deny it, the more Pellea tries to hold him off, the deeper his desire goes. And once he realizes she is carrying his child, he knows there is no turning back. They make their way through the castle corridors, exploring secret rooms, tricking guards, attending a masked ball and stealing a prized artifact, but when Monte escapes along an ancient passageway, Pellea refuses to go with him. She's torn between her love for Monte and her devotion to her dying father. Will she be caught up in the coming war and pay the ultimate price for her divided loyalties?

Well, you know the drill—you'll have to read the book to find out! I hope you enjoy it.

All the best,

Raye Morgan

RAYE MORGAN
Crown Prince, Pregnant Bride!

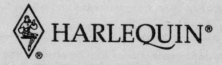

TORONTO • NEW YORK • LONDON
AMSTERDAM • PARIS • SYDNEY • HAMBURG
STOCKHOLM • ATHENS • TOKYO • MILAN • MADRID
PRAGUE • WARSAW • BUDAPEST • AUCKLAND

Recycling programs
for this product may
not exist in your area.

ISBN-13: 978-0-373-17703-5

CROWN PRINCE, PREGNANT BRIDE!

First North American Publication 2011

Raye Morgan has been a nursery-school teacher, a travel agent, a clerk and a business editor, but her best job ever has been writing romances—and fostering romance in her own family at the same time. Current score: two boys married, two more to go. Raye has published more than seventy romances and claims to have many more waiting in the wings. She lives in Southern California with her husband and whichever son happens to be staying at home at that moment.

This book is dedicated to Baby Kate

CHAPTER ONE

THOUGH MONTE COULDN'T see her, Pellea Marallis passed so close to the Crown Prince's hiding place, he easily caught a hint of her intoxicating perfume. That gave him an unexpected jolt. It brought back a panoply of memories, like flipping through the pages of a book—a vision of sunlight shining through a gauzy white dress, silhouetting a slim, beautifully rounded female form, a flashing picture of drops of water cascading like a thousand diamonds onto creamy silken skin, a sense of cool satin sheets and caresses that set his flesh on fire.

He bit down hard on his lower lip to stop the wave of sensuality that threatened to wash over him. He wasn't here to renew the romance. He was here to kidnap her. And he wasn't about to let that beguiling man-woman thing get in the way this time.

She passed close again and he could hear the rustle of her long skirt as it brushed against the wall he was leaning on. She was pacing back and forth in her courtyard, a garden retreat built right into this side of the castle, giving her a small lush forest where she spent most of her time. The surrounding rooms—a huge closet filled with clothes and a small sitting room, a neighboring compact office stacked to the ceiling with books, a sumptuously decorated bedroom—each opened onto the courtyard with French doors, making her living space a mixture of indoors and outdoors in an enchanting maze of exciting colors and provocative scents.

She was living like a princess.

Did he resent it all? Of course. How could he not?

But this was not the side of the castle where his family had lived before the overthrow of their royal rule. That area had been burned the night his parents were murdered by the Granvillis, the thugs who still ruled Ambria, this small island country that had once been home to his family. He understood that part of the castle was only now being renovated, twenty-five years later.

And that he resented.

But Pellea had nothing to do with the way his family had been robbed of their birthright. He had no intention of holding her accountable. Her father was another matter. His long-time status as the Grand Counselor to the Granvillis was what gave Pellea the right to live in this luxury—and his treachery twenty-five years ago was considered a subject of dusty history.

Not to Monte. But that was a matter for another time.

He hadn't seen her yet. He'd slipped into the dressing room as soon as he'd emerged from the secret passageway. And now he was just biding his time before he revealed his presence.

He was taking this slowly, because no matter what

he'd told himself, she affected him in ways no other woman ever had. In fact, she'd been known to send his restraint reeling, and he knew he had to take this at a cautious pace if he didn't want things to spin out of control again.

He heard her voice and his head rose. Listening hard, he tried to figure out if she had someone with her. No. She was talking on her mobile, and when she turned in his direction, he could just make out what she was saying.

"Seed pearls of course. And little pink rosebuds. I think that ought to do it."

He wasn't really listening to the words. Just the sound of her had him mesmerized. He'd never noticed before how appealing her voice was, just as an instrument. He hadn't heard it for some time, and it caught the ear the way a lilting acoustic guitar solo might, each note crisp, crystal clear and sweet in a way that touched the soul.

As she talked, he listened to the sound and smiled. He wanted to see her and the need was growing in him.

But to do that, he would have to move to a riskier position so that he could see out through the open French doors. Though he'd slipped easily into her huge dressing room, he needed to move to a niche beside a tall wardrobe where he could see everything without being seen himself. Carefully, he made his move.

And there she was. His heart was thudding so hard, he could barely breathe.

The thing about Pellea, and part of the reason she so completely captivated him, was that she seemed to embody a sense of royal command even though there wasn't a royal bone in her body. She was classically beautiful, like a Greek statue, only slimmer, like an angel in a Renaissance painting, only earthier, like a dancer drawn by Toulouse-Lautrec, only more graceful, like a thirties-era film star, only more mysteriously luminescent. She was all a woman could be and still be of this earth.

Barely.

To a casual glance, she looked like a normal woman. Her face was exceptionally pretty, but there were others with dark eyes as almond-shaped, with long, lustrous lashes that seemed to sweep the air. Her hair floated about her face like a misty cloud of spun gold and her form was trim and nicely rounded. Her lips were red and full and inviting. Perfection.

But there were others who had much the same advantages. Others had caught his eye through the years, but not many had filled his mind and touched off the sense of longing that she had.

There was something more to Pellea, something in the dignity with which she held herself, an inner fire that burned behind a certain sadness in her eyes, an inner drive, a sense of purpose, that set her apart. She could be playful as a kitten one minute, then smoldering with a provocative allure, and just as suddenly, aflame with righteous anger.

From the moment he'd first seen her, he'd known she was special. And for a few days two months ago, she'd been his.

"Didn't I give you my sketches?" she was saying into the phone. "I tend to lean a little more toward tradi-tional. Not too modern. No off-the-shoulder stuff. Not for this."

He frowned, wondering what on earth she was talk-ing about. Designing a ball gown maybe? He could see her on the dance floor, drawing all eyes. Would he ever get the chance to dance with her? Not in a ballroom, but maybe here, in her courtyard. Why not?

It was a beautiful setting. When he'd been here before, it had been winter and everything had been lifeless and stark. But spring was here now, and the space was a riot of color.

A fountain spilled water in the center of the area, making music that was a pleasant, tinkling background. Tiled pathways meandered through the area, weaving in among rosebushes and tropical plants, palms and a small bamboo forest.

Yes, they would have to turn on some music and dance. He could almost feel her in his arms. He stole another glance at her, at the way she held her long, grace-ful neck, at the way her free hand fluttered like a bird as she made her point, at the way her dressing gown gaped open, revealing the lacy shift she wore underneath.

"Diamonds?" she was saying into the phone. "Oh, no. No diamonds. Just the one, of course. That's customary. I'm not really a shower-me-with-diamonds sort of girl, you know what I mean?"

He reached out and just barely touched the fluttering hem of her flowing sleeve as she passed. She turned quickly, as though she'd sensed something, but he'd pulled back just in time and she didn't see him. He smiled, pleased with himself. He would let her know he was here when he was good and ready.

"As I remember it, the veil is more of an ivory shade. There are seed pearls scattered all over the crown area, and then down along the edges on both sides. I think that will be enough."

Veil? Monte frowned. Finally, a picture swam into stark relief and he realized what she must be talking about. It sounded like a wedding. She was planning her wedding ensemble.

She was getting married.

He stared at her, appalled. What business did she have getting married? Had she forgotten all about him so quickly? Anger curled through him like smoke and he only barely held back the impulse to stride out and confront her.

She couldn't get married. He wouldn't allow it.

And yet, he realized with a twinge of conscience, it wasn't as though he was planning to marry her himself. Of course not. He had bigger fish to fry. He had an invasion to orchestrate and manage. Besides, there was no way he would ever marry the daughter of the biggest betrayer still alive of his family—the DeAngelis Royalty.

And yet, to think she was planning to marry someone else so soon after their time together burned like a scorpion's sting.

What the hell!

A muted gong sounded, making him jerk in surprise. That was new. There had been a brass knocker a few weeks ago. What else had she changed since he'd been here before?

Getting married—hah! It was a good thing he'd shown up to kidnap her just in time.

Pellea had just rung off with her clothing designer, and she raised her head at the sound of her new entry gong. She sighed, shoulders drooping. The last thing she wanted was company, and she was afraid she knew who this was anyway. Her husband-to-be. Oh, joy.

"Enter," she called out.

There was a heavy metal clang as the gate was pulled open and then the sound of boots on the tile. A tall man entered, his neatly trimmed hair too short to identify the color, but cut close to his perfectly formed head. His shoulders were wide, his body neatly proportioned and very fit-looking. His long face would have been handsome if he could have trained himself to get rid of the perpetual sneer he wore like a mark of superiority at all times.

Leonardo Granvilli was the oldest son of Georges Granvilli, leader of the rebellion that had taken over this island nation twenty-five years before, the man who now ruled as *The General*, a term that somewhat softened the edges of his relatively despotic regime.

"My darling," Leonardo said coolly in a deep, sonorous voice. "You're radiant as the dawn on this beautiful day."

"Oh, spare me, Leonardo," she said dismissively. Her tone held casual disregard but wasn't in any way meant to offend. "No need for empty words of praise. We've known each other since we were children. I think by now we've taken the measure, each of the other. I don't need a daily snow job."

Leonardo made a guttural sound in his throat and threw a hand up to cover his forehead in annoyance. "Pellea, why can't you be like other women and just accept the phony flattery for what it is? It's nothing but form, darling. A way to get through the awkward moments. A little sugar to help the medicine go down."

Pellea laughed shortly, but cut it off almost before it had begun. Pretending to be obedient, she went into mock royal mode for him.

"Pray tell me, kind sir, what brings my noble knight to my private chambers on such a day as this?"

He actually smiled. "That's more like it."

She curtsied low and long and his smile widened.

"Bravo. This marriage may just work out after all."

Her glare shot daggers his way, as though to say, *In your dreams*, but he ignored that.

"I came with news. We may have to postpone our wedding."

"What?" Involuntarily, her hands went to her belly—and the moment she realized what she'd done, she snatched them away again. "Why?"

"That old fool, the last duke of the DeAngelis clan, has finally died. This means a certain level of upheaval is probable in the expatriate Ambrian community. They will have to buzz about and try to find a new patriarch, it seems. We need to be alert and ready to move on any sort of threat that might occur to our regime."

"Do you expect anything specific?"

He shook his head. "Not really. Just the usual gnashing of teeth and bellowing of threats. We can easily handle it."

She frowned, shaking her head. "Then why postpone? Why not move the date up instead?"

He reached out and tousled her hair. "Ah, my little buttercup. So eager to be wed."

She pushed his hand away, then turned toward the fountain in the middle of the courtyard and shrugged elaborately. "'If it were done when 'tis done, then 'twere well it were done quickly,'" she muttered darkly.

"What's that my sweet?" he said, following into the sunshine.

"Nothing." She turned back to face him. "I will, of course, comply with your wishes. But for my own purposes, a quick wedding would be best."

He nodded, though his eyes were hooded. "I understand. Your father's condition and all that." He shrugged. "I'll talk to my father and we'll hit upon a date, I'm sure." His gaze flickered over her and he smiled. "To think that after all this time, and all the effort you've always gone to in putting me off, I'm finally going to end up with the woman of my dreams." He almost seemed to tear up a bit. "It restores one's faith, doesn't it?"

"Absolutely." She couldn't help but smile back at him, though she was shaking her head at the same time. "Oh,

Leonardo, I sometimes think it would be better if you found someone to love."

He looked shocked. "What are you talking about? You know very well you've always been my choice."

"I said *love*," she retorted. "Not *desire to possess*."

He shrugged. "To each his own."

Pellea sighed but she was still smiling.

Monte watched this exchange while cold anger spread through him like a spell, turning him from a normal man into something akin to a raging monster. And yet, he didn't move a muscle. He stood frozen, as though cast in stone. Only his mind and his emotions were alive.

And his hatred. He hated Leonardo, hated Leonardo's father, hated his entire family.

Bit by bit, the anger was banked and set aside to smolder. He was experienced enough to know white-hot emotional ire led to mistakes every time. He wouldn't make any mistakes. He needed to keep his head clear and his emotions in check.

All of them, good and bad.

One step at a time, he made himself relax. His body control was exceptional and he used it now. He wanted to keep cool so that he would catch the exact right time to strike. It wouldn't be now. That would be foolish. But it would be soon.

He hadn't been prepared for something like this. The time he and Pellea had spent together just a few weeks before had been magical. He'd been hungry to see her again, aching to touch her, eager to catch her lips with his and feel that soaring sense of wonder again. He had promised himself there would be no lovemaking to distract him this time—but he'd been kidding himself. The moment he saw her he knew he had to have her in his arms again.

That was all. Nothing serious, nothing permanent. A part of him had known she would have to marry someone—eventually. But still, to think that she would marry this…this…

Words failed him.

"I'd like you to come down to the library. We need to look at the plans for the route to the retreat in the gilded carriage after we are joined as one," Leonardo was saying.

"No honeymoon," she said emphatically, raising both hands as though to emphasize her words. "I told you that from the beginning."

He looked startled, but before he could protest, she went on.

"As long as my father is ill, I won't leave Ambria."

He sighed, making a face but seemingly reconciled to her decision. "People will think it strange," he noted.

"Let them."

She knew that disappointed him but it couldn't be helped. Right now her father was everything to her. He had been her rock all her life, the only human being in this world she could fully trust and believe in and she wasn't about to abandon him now.

Still, she needed this marriage. Leonardo understood

why and was willing to accept the terms she'd agreed
to this on. Everything was ready, the wheels had begun
to turn, the path was set. As long as nothing got in the
way, she should be married within the next week. Until
then, she could only hope that nothing would happen to
upset the apple cart.

"I'll come with you," she said. "Just give me a minute
to do a quick change into something more suitable."

She turned and stepped into her dressing room, pulling the door closed behind her. Moving quickly, she
opened her gown and began unbuttoning her lacy dress
from the neck down. And then she caught sight of his
boots. Her fingers froze on the buttons as she stared at
the boots. Her head snapped up and her dark eyes met
Monte's brilliant blue gaze. Every sinew constructing
her body went numb.

She was much more than shocked. She was horrified.
As the implications of this visit came into focus, she
had to clasp her free hand over her mouth to keep from
letting out a shriek. For just a moment, she went into a
tailspin and could barely keep her balance.

Eyes wide, she stared at him. A thousand thoughts
ricocheted through her, bouncing like ping-pong balls
against her emotions. Anger, remorse, resentment, joy—
even love—they were all there and all aimed straight into
those gorgeous blue eyes, rapid-fire. If looks could kill,
he would be lying on the floor, shot through the heart.

A part of her was tempted to turn on her heel, summon
Leonardo and be done with it. Because she knew as

sure as she knew her own name that this would all end badly.

Monte couldn't be a part of her life. There was no way she could even admit to anyone here in the castle that she knew him. All she had to do was have Leonardo call the guard, and it would be over. They would dispose of him. She would never see him again—never have to think about him again, never again have to cry into her pillow until it was a soggy sponge.

But she knew that was all just bravado. She would never, ever do anything to hurt him if she could help it.

He gave her a crooked grin as though to say, "Didn't you know I'd be back?"

No, she didn't know. She hadn't known. And she still didn't want to believe it. She didn't say a word.

Quickly, she turned and looked out into the courtyard. Leonardo was waiting patiently, humming a little tune as he looked at the fountain. Biting her lower lip, she turned and managed to stagger out of the dressing room towards him, stumbling a bit and panting for breath.

"What is it?" he said in alarm, stepping forward to catch her by the shoulders. He'd obviously noted that she was uncharacteristically disheveled. "Are you all right?"

"No." She flickered a glance his way, thinking fast, then took a deep breath and shook her head. "No. Migraine."

"Oh, no." He looked puzzled, but concerned.

She pulled away from his grip on her shoulders, regaining her equilibrium with effort.

"I...I'm sorry, but I don't think I can come with you right now. I can hardly even think straight."

"But you were fine thirty seconds ago," he noted, completely at sea.

"Migraines come on fast," she told him, putting a hand to the side of her head and wincing. "But a good lie-down will fix me up. How about...after tea?" She looked at him earnestly. "I'll meet you then. Say, five o'clock?"

Leonardo frowned, but he nodded. "All right. I've got a tennis match at three, so that will work out fine." He looked at her with real concern, but just a touch of wariness.

"I hope this won't affect your ability to go to the ball tonight."

"Oh, no, of course not."

"Everyone is expecting our announcement to be made there. And you will be wearing the tiara, won't you?"

She waved him away. "Leonardo, don't worry. I'll be wearing the tiara and all will be as planned. I should be fine by tonight."

"Good." He still seemed wary. "But you should see Dr. Dracken. I'll send him up."

"No!" She shook her head. "I just need to rest. Give me a few hours. I'll be good as new."

He studied her for a moment, then shrugged. "As you wish." He bent over her hand like a true suitor. "Until we meet again, my beloved betrothed."

She nodded, almost pushing him toward the gate. "Likewise, I'm sure," she said out of the corner of her mouth.

"Pip pip." And he was off.

She waited until she heard the outer gate clang, then turned like a fury and marched back into the dressing room. She ripped open the door and glared at Monte with a look in her eyes that should have frozen the blood in his veins.

"How dare you? How dare you do this?"

Her vehemence was actually throwing him off his game a bit. He had expected a little more joy at seeing him again. He was enjoying the sight of her. Why couldn't she feel the same?

She really was a feast for the senses. Her eyes were bright—even if that seemed to be anger for the moment—and her cheeks were smudged pink.

"How dare you do this to me again?" she demanded.

"This isn't like before," he protested. "This is totally different."

"Really? Here you are, sneaking into my country, just like before. Here you are, hiding in my chambers again. Just like before."

His smile was meant to be beguiling. "But this time, when I leave, you're going with me."

She stared at him, hating him and loving him at the same time. Going with him! What a dream that was. She could no more go with him than she could swim the channel. If only…

For just a split second, she allowed herself to give in to her emotions. If only things were different. How she would love to throw herself into his arms and hold him tight, to feel his hard face against hers, to sense his heart pound as his interest quickened…

But she couldn't do that. She couldn't even think about it. She'd spent too many nights dreaming of him, dreaming of his tender touch. She had to forget all that. Too many lives depended on her. She couldn't let him see the slightest crack in her armor.

And most of all, she couldn't let him know about the baby.

"How did you get in here?" she demanded coldly. "Oh, wait. Don't even try to tell me. You'll just lie."

The provocative expression in his eyes changed to ice in an instant.

"Pellea, I'm not a liar," he said in a low, urgent tone. "I'll tell you or I won't, but what I say will be the truth as I know it every time. Count on it."

Their gazes locked in mutual indignation. Pellea was truly angry with him for showing up like this, for complicating her life and endangering them both, and yet she knew she was using that anger as a shield. If he touched her, she would surely melt. Just looking at him did enough damage to her determined stance.

Why did he have to be so beautiful? With his dark hair and shocking blue eyes, he had film-star looks, but that wasn't all. He was tall, muscular, strong in a way that would make any woman swoon. He looked tough, capable of holding his own in a fight, and yet there was nothing cocky about him. He had a quiet confidence that made any form of showing off unnecessary. You just knew by looking at him that he was ready for any challenge—physical or intellectual.

But how about emotional? Despite all his strength, there was a certain sensitivity deep in his blue eyes. The sort of hint of vulnerability only a woman might notice. Or was that just hopeful dreaming on her part?

"Never mind all that," she said firmly. "We've got to get you out of here."

His anger drifted away like morning fog and his eyes were smiling again. "After I've gone to so much trouble to get in?"

Oh, please don't smile at me! she begged silently. This was difficult enough without this charm offensive clouding her mind. She glared back.

"You are going. This very moment would be a good time to do it."

His gaze caressed her cheek. "How can I leave now that I've found you again?"

She gritted her teeth. "You're not going to mesmerize me like you did last time. You're not staying here at all." She pointed toward the gate. "I want you to go."

He raised one dark eyebrow and made no move toward the door. "You going to call the guard?"

Her eyes blazed at him. "If I have to."

He looked pained. "Actually, I'd rather you didn't."

"Then you'd better go, hadn't you?"

He sighed and managed to look as though he regretted all this. "I can't leave yet. Not without what I came for."

She threw up her hands. "That has nothing to do with me."

His smile was back. "That's where you're wrong. You see, it's you that I came for. How do you feel about a good old-fashioned kidnapping?"

CHAPTER TWO

PELLEA BLINKED QUICKLY, but that was the only sign she allowed to show his words had shocked her—rocked her, actually, to the point where she almost needed to reach out and hold on to something to keep from falling over.

Monte had come to kidnap her? Was he joking? Or was he crazy?

"Really?" With effort, she managed to fill her look with mock disdain. "How do you propose to get me past all the guards and barriers? How do you think you'll manage that without someone noticing? Especially when I'll be fighting you every step of the way and creating a scene and doing everything else I can think of to ruin your silly kidnapping scheme?"

"I've got a plan." He favored her with a knowing grin.

"Oh, I see." Eyes wide, she turned with a shrug, as though asking the world to judge him. "He's got a plan. Say no more."

He followed her. "You scoff, Pellea. But you'll soon see things my way."

She whirled to face him and her gaze sharpened as she remembered his last visit. "How do you get in here, anyway? You've never explained that." She shook her head, considering him from another angle. "There are guards everywhere. How do you get past them?"

His grin widened. "Secrets of the trade, my dear."

"And just what is your trade these days?" she asked archly. "Second-story man?"

"No, Pellea." His grin faded. Now they were talking about serious things. "Actually, I still consider myself the royal heir to the Ambrian throne."

She rolled her eyes. "Good luck with that one."

He turned and met her gaze with an intensity that burned. "I'm the Crown Prince of Ambria. Hadn't you heard? I thought you understood that."

She stared back at him. "That's over," she said softly, searching his eyes. "Long over."

He shook his head slowly, his blue eyes burning with a surreal light. "No. It's real and it's now. And very soon, the world will know it."

Fear gripped her heart. What he was suggesting was war. People she loved would be hurt. And yet…

Reaching out, she touched him, forgetting her vow not to. She flattened her palm against his chest and felt his heartbeat, felt the heat and the flesh of him.

"Oh, please, Monte," she whispered, her eyes filled with the sadness of a long future of suffering. "Please, don't…"

He took her hand and brought it to his lips, kissing the center of her palm without losing his hold on her gaze for a moment. "I won't let anything hurt you," he promised, though he knew he might as well whistle into the wind. Once his operation went into action, all bets would be off. "You know that."

She shook her head, rejecting what he'd said. "No, Monte, I don't know that. You plan to come in here and rip our lives apart. Once you start a revolution, you start a fire in the people and you can't control where that fire will burn. There will be pain and agony on all sides. There always is."

His shrug was elaborate on purpose. "There was pain and agony that night twenty-five years ago when my mother and my father were killed by the Granvillis. When I and my brothers and sisters were spirited off into the night and told to forget we were royal. In one fire-ravaged night, we lost our home, our kingdom, our destiny and our parents." His head went back and he winced as though the pain was still fresh. "What do you want me to do? Forgive those who did that to me and mine?"

A look of pure determination froze his face into the mask of a warrior. "I'll never do that. They need to pay."

She winced. Fear gripped her heart. She knew what this meant. Her own beloved father was counted among Monte's enemies. But she also knew that he was strong and determined, and he meant what he threatened. Wasn't there any way she could stop this from happening?

The entry gong sounded, making them both jump.

"Yes?" she called out, hiding her alarm.

"Excuse me, Miss Marallis," a voice called in. "It's Sergeant Fromer. I just wanted to check what time you wanted us to bring the tiara by."

"The guard," she whispered, looking at Monte sharply. "I should ask him in right now."

He held her gaze. "But you won't," he said softly.

She stared at him for a long moment. She wanted with all her heart to prove him wrong. She should do it. It would be so easy, wouldn't it?

"Miss?" the guard called in again.

"Uh, sorry, Sergeant Fromer." She looked at Monte again and knew she wouldn't do it. She shook her head, ashamed of herself. "About seven would be best," she called to him. "The hairdresser should be here by then."

"Will do. Thank you, miss."

And he was gone, carrying with him all hope for sanity. She stared at the area of the gate.

There it was—another chance to do the right thing and rid herself of this menace to her peace of mind forever. Why couldn't she follow through? She turned and looked at Monte, her heart sinking. Was she doomed? Not if she stayed strong. This couldn't be like it was before. She'd been vulnerable the last time. She'd just had the horrible fight with her father that she had been dreading for years, and when Monte had jumped into her life, she was in the mood to do dangerous things.

The first time she'd seen him, he'd appeared seemingly out of nowhere and found her sobbing beside her fountain. She'd just come back to her chambers from that

fight and she'd been sick at heart, hating that she'd hurt
the man she loved most in the world—her father. And
so afraid that she would have to do what he wanted her
to do anyway.

Her father's health had begun to fade at that point,
but he wasn't bedridden yet, as he was now. He'd sum-
moned her to his room and told her in no uncertain
terms that he expected her to marry Leonardo. And
she'd told him in similar fashion that she would have
to be dragged kicking and screaming to the altar. No
other way would work. He'd called her an ungrateful
child and had brought up the fact that she was looking to
be an old maid soon if she didn't get herself a husband.
She'd called him an overbearing parent and threatened
to marry the gardener.

That certainly got a response, but it was mainly nega-
tive and she regretted having said such a thing now. But
he'd been passionate, almost obsessive about the need
for her to marry Leonardo.

"Marry the man. You've known him all your life. You
get along fine. He wants you, and as his wife, you'll have
so much power…"

"Power!" she'd responded with disdain. "All you care
about is power."

His face had gone white. "Power is important," he
told her in a clipped, hard voice. "As much as you may
try to pretend otherwise, it rules our lives." And then,
haltingly, he'd told her the story of what had happened
to her mother—the real story this time, not the one she'd
grown up believing.

"Victor Halma wanted her," he said, naming the man who had been the Granvillis' top enforcer when Pellea was a very small child.

"Wha-what do you mean?" she'd stammered. There was a sick feeling in the pit of her stomach and she was afraid she understood only too well.

"He was always searching her out in the halls, showing up unexpectedly whenever she thought she was safe. He wouldn't leave her alone. She was in a panic."

She closed her eyes and murmured, "My poor mother."

"There was still a lot of hostility toward me because I had worked with the DeAngelis royal family before the revolution," he went on. "I wasn't trusted then as I am now. I tried to fight him, but it was soon apparent I had no one on my side." He drew in a deep breath. "I was sent on a business trip to Paris. He made his move while I was gone."

"Father…"

"You see, I had no power." His face, already pale, took on a haggard look. "I couldn't refuse to go. And once I was gone, he forced her to go to his quarters."

Pellea gasped, shivering as though an icy blast had swept into the room.

"She tried to run away, but he had the guard drag her into his chamber and lock her in. And there, while she was waiting, she found a knife and killed herself before he could…" His voice trailed off.

Pellea's hands clutched her throat. "You always told me she died during an influenza epidemic," she choked out. She was overwhelmed with this news, and yet, deep down, she'd always known there was something she wasn't being told.

He nodded. "That was what I told you. That was what I told everyone. And there was an epidemic at the time. But she didn't die of influenza. She died of shame."

Pellea swayed. The room seemed to dip and swerve around her. "And the man?" she asked hoarsely.

"He had an unfortunate accident soon after," her father said dryly, making it clear he wasn't about to go into details. "But you understand me, don't you? You see the position we were in? That's what happens when you don't have power."

"Or when you work for horrible people," she shot back passionately.

Shaking his head, he almost smiled. "The strange thing was, the Granvillis started to trust me after that. I moved up in the ranks. I gained power." He looked at his daughter sternly. "Today, nothing like that could happen to me. And what I want for you is that same sort of immunity from harm."

She understood what he wanted for her. She ached with love for him, ached for what he'd gone through, ached for what her own mother had endured. Her heart broke for them all.

But she still hadn't been able to contemplate marrying Leonardo. Not then.

To some degree, she could relate to his obsession to get and hold power. Still, it was his obsession, not hers and she had no interest in making the sort of down payment on a sense of control that marrying Leonardo would entail.

But this had been the condition she'd been in when she'd first looked up and found Monte standing in her courtyard. She knew she'd never seen him before, and that was unusual. This was a small country and most in the castle had been there for years. You tended to know everyone you ran into, at least by sight. She'd jumped up and looked toward the gate, as though to run.

But he'd smiled. Something in that smile captivated her every time, and it had all begun that afternoon.

"Hi," he'd said. "I'm running from some castle guards. Mind if I hide in here?"

Even as he spoke, she heard the guards at the gate. And just that quickly, she became a renegade.

"Hurry, hide in there," she'd said, pointing to her bedroom. "Behind the bookcase." She'd turned toward the gate. "I'll deal with the guards."

And so began her life as an accomplice to a criminal—and so also her infatuation with the most wrong man she could have fallen in love with.

Monte didn't really appreciate the effort all this had cost her. He'd taken it for granted that she would send the guard away. She'd done the same thing the last time he was here—and that had been more dangerous for them both—because they'd already seen him in the halls at that point. The whole castle was turned upside down for the next two days as they hunted for him. And the entire time, she'd had him hidden in her bedroom.

No one knew he was here now except Pellea—so far.

"Was that the DeAngelis tiara you were talking about just now?" he asked her. "I thought I heard Leonardo bring it up."

She glared at him. "How long have you been here spying on me? What else did you hear?"

He raised an eyebrow. "What else didn't you want me to hear?"

She threw her hands up.

"Don't worry," he said. "The wedding-dress-design discussion and your talk with Leonardo were about it."

They both turned to look at the beautiful gown hanging against a tall, mahogany wardrobe. "Is this the gown you're wearing to the ball tonight?"

"Yes."

It was stunning. Black velvet swirled against deep green satin. It hung before him looking as though it was already filled with a warm, womanly body. Reaching out, he spanned the waist of it with his hands and imagined dancing with her.

"The DeAngelis tiara will look spectacular with this," he told her.

"Do you remember what it looks like?" she asked in surprise.

"Not in great detail. But I've seen pictures." He gave her a sideways look of irony. "My mother's tiara."

She shivered, pulling her arms in close about her. "It hasn't been your mother's tiara for a long, long time," she said, wishing she didn't sound so defensive.

He nodded slowly. "My mother's and that of every

other queen of Ambria going back at least three centuries," he added softly, almost to himself.

She shivered again. "I'm sure you're right."

His smile was humorless. "To the victor go the spoils."

"I didn't make the rules." Inside, she groaned. Still defensive. But she did feel the guilt of the past. How could she not?

"And yet, it will take more than twenty-five years to erase the memories that are centuries old. Memories of what my family accomplished here."

She bit her lip, then looked at him, looked at the sense of tragedy in his beautiful blue eyes, and felt the tug on her heart.

"I'm sorry," she said quickly, reaching for him and putting a hand on his upper arm. "I'm sorry that I have to wear your mother's tiara. They've asked me to do it and I said yes."

He covered her hand with his own and turned toward her. She recognized the light in his eyes and knew he wanted to kiss her. Her pulse raced, but she couldn't let it happen. Quickly, she pulled away.

He sighed, shaking his head in regret, but his mind was still on something else.

"Where is it?" he asked, looking around the wardrobe. "Where do you keep it?"

"The tiara?" She searched his eyes. What was he thinking? "It's in its case in the museum room, where it always is. Didn't you hear Sergeant Fromer? The guards will bring it to me just before I leave for the ball. And they will accompany me to the ballroom. The tiara is under guard at all times."

He nodded, eyeing her speculatively. "And so shall you be, once you put it on."

"I imagine so."

He nodded again, looking thoughtful. "I was just reading an article about it the other day," he said, half musing. "Diamonds, rubies, emeralds, all huge and of superior quality. Not to mention the wonderful craftsmanship of the tiara itself. It's estimated to be worth more than some small countries are."

Suddenly she drew her breath in. She hadn't known him long, but she was pretty sure she knew a certain side of him all too well.

"Oh, no you don't!" she cried, all outrage.

He looked at her in surprise. "What?"

She glared at him. "You're thinking about grabbing it, aren't you?"

"The tiara?" He stared at her for a moment and then he threw his head back and laughed. That was actually a fabulous idea. He liked the way she thought.

"Pellea," he said, taking her by the shoulders and dropping a kiss on her forehead. "You are perfection itself. You can't marry Leonardo."

She shivered. She couldn't help it. His touch was like agony and ecstasy, all rolled into one. But she kept her head about her.

"Who shall I marry then?" she responded quickly. "Are you ready to give me an offer?"

He stared at her, not responding. How could he say

anything? He couldn't make her an offer. He couldn't marry her. And anyway, he might be dead by the end of the summer.

Besides, there was another factor. If he was going to be ruler of Ambria, could he marry the daughter of his family's biggest betrayer? Not likely.

"I think kidnapping will work out better," he told her, and he wasn't joking.

She'd known he would say that, or something similar. She knew he was attracted to her. That, he couldn't hide. But she was a realist and she also knew he hated her father and the current regime with which she was allied. How could it be any other way? He could talk about taking her with him all he wanted, she knew there was no future for her there.

"I'll fight you all the way," she said flatly.

He smiled down into her fierce eyes. "There's always the best option, of course."

"And what is that?"

"That you come with me willingly."

She snorted. "Right. Before or after I marry Leonardo?"

He looked pained. "I can't believe you're serious."

She raised her chin and glared at him. "I am marrying Leonardo in four days. I hope."

He brushed the stray hairs back off her cheek and his fingers lingered, caressing her silken skin. "But why?" he asked softly.

"Because I want to," she responded stoutly. "I've promised I will do it and I mean to keep that promise."

Resolutely, she turned away from him and began searching through a clothes rack, looking for the clothes she meant to change into.

He came up behind her. "Is it because of your father?"

She whirled and stared at him. "Leave my father out of this."

"Ah-hah. So it is your father."

She turned back to searching through the hangers. He watched her for a moment, thinking that he'd never known a woman whose movements were so fluid. Every move she made was almost a part of a dance. And watching her turned him on in ways that were bound to cripple his ability to think clearly. He shook his head. He couldn't let that happen, not if he wanted to succeed here.

"Leonardo," he scoffed. "Please. Why Leonardo?"

Unconsciously, she cupped her hand over her belly. There was a tiny baby growing inside. He must never know that. He was the last person she could tell—ever. "It's my father's fondest wish."

"Because he might become ruler of Ambria?"

"Yes." How could she deny it? "And because he asked."

That set him back a moment. "What if I asked?" he ventured.

She turned to him, but his eyes showed nothing that could give her any hope. "Ah, but you won't, will you?"

He looked away. "Probably not."

"There's your answer."

"Where is Georges?" he asked, naming the Granvilli who had killed his parents. "What does he say about all this?"

She hesitated, choosing her words carefully. "The General seems to be unwell right now. I'm not sure what the specific problem is, but he's resting in the seaside villa at Grapevine Bay. Leonardo has been taking over more and more of the responsibilities of power himself." She raised her head and looked him squarely in the eye. "And the work seems to suit him."

"Does it? I hope he's enjoying himself. He won't have much longer to do that, as I intend to take that job away from him shortly."

She threw up her hands, not sure if he meant it or if this was just typical male bombast. "What exactly do you mean to do?" she asked, trying to pin him down.

He looked at her and smiled, coming closer, touching her hair with one hand.

"Nothing that you need to worry about."

But his thoughts were not nearly as sanguine as he pretended. She really had no conception of how deep his anger lay and how his hatred had eaten away at him for most of his life. Ever since that night when the castle had burned and his parents were murdered by the Granvilli clan. Payment was due. Retribution was pending.

"Is your father really very ill?" he asked quietly.

"Yes." She found the shirt she wanted and pulled it down.

"And you want to make him happy before he…"

He swallowed his next words even before she snapped her head around and ordered curtly, "Don't say it!"

He bit his tongue. That was a stupid thing to have thought, even if he never actually got the words out. He didn't mind annoying her about things he didn't think she should care so much about, but to annoy her about her father was just plain counterproductive.

"Well, he would like to see you become the future first lady of the land, wouldn't he?" he amended lamely.

He tried to think of what he knew about her father. Marallis had been considered an up-and-coming advisor in his own father's regime. From what he'd been able to glean, the king had recognized his superior abilities and planned to place him in a top job. And then the rebellion had swept over them, and it turned out Vaneck Marallis had signed on with the other side. Was it any wonder he should feel betrayed by the man? He was the enemy. He very likely gave the rebels the inside information they needed to win the day. There was no little corner of his heart that had any intention of working on forgiveness for the man.

"Okay, it's getting late," she said impatiently. "I have to go check on my father."

"Because he's ill?"

"Because he's very ill." She knew she needed to elaborate, but when she tried to speak, her throat choked and she had to pause, waiting for her voice to clear again. "I always go in to see him for a few minutes at this time in the afternoon." She looked at him. "When I get back, we'll have to decide what I'm going to do with you."

"Will we?" His grin was ample evidence of his opinion on the matter, but she turned away and didn't bother to challenge him.

Going to her clothes rack, she pulled out a trim, cream-colored linen suit with slacks and a crisp jacket and slipped behind a privacy screen to change into them. He watched as she emerged, looking quietly efficient and good at whatever job she might be attempting. And ravishingly beautiful at the same time. He'd never known another woman who impressed him as much as this one did. Once again he had a pressing urge to find a way to take her with him.

It wouldn't be impossible. She thought he would have to get her past the guards, but she was wrong. He had his own way into the castle and he could easily get her out. But only if she was at least halfway cooperative. It was up to him to convince her to be.

"I don't have time to decide what to do with you right now," she told him, her gaze hooded as she met his eyes. "I have to go check on my father, and it's getting late. You stay here and hold down the fort. I'll be back in about half an hour."

"I may be here," he offered casually. "Or not."

She hesitated. She didn't like that answer. "Tell me now, are you going to stay here and wait, or are you going to go looking for Leonardo and get killed?" she demanded of him.

He laughed shortly. "I think I can handle myself around your so-called fiancé," he said dismissively.

Her gaze sharpened and she looked seriously into his

eyes. "Watch out for Leonardo. He'll kill you without batting an eye."

"Are you serious? That prancing prig?"

She shook her head. "Don't be fooled by his veneer of urbanity. He's hard as nails. When I suggested you might be killed, I meant it."

He searched her eyes for evidence that she really cared. It was there, much as she tried to hide it. He smiled.

"I'm not too keen on the 'killed' part. But as for the rest…"

She glanced at her watch. Time was fleeting. "I'm running out of time," she told him. "Go out and wait in the courtyard. I just have one last thing to check."

"What's that?" he asked.

She looked pained. "None of your business. I do have my privacy to maintain. Now go out and wait."

He walked out into the lush courtyard and heard the door click shut behind him. Turning, he could see her through the glass door, walking back into her closet again. Probably changed her mind on what to wear, he thought to himself. And he had a twinge of regret. He didn't have all that much time here and he hated to think of missing a moment with her.

Did that mean he'd given up on the kidnapping? No. Not at all. Still, there was more to this trip than just seeing Pellea.

He scanned the courtyard and breathed in the atmosphere. The castle of his ancestors was all around him.

For a few minutes, he thought about his place in history. Would he be able to restore the monarchy? Would he bring his family back to their rightful place, where they should have been all along?

Of course he would. He didn't allow doubts. His family belonged here and he would see that it happened. He'd already found two of his brothers, part of the group of "Lost Royals" who had escaped when the castle was burned and had hidden from the wrath of the Granvillis ever since. There were two more brothers and two sisters he hadn't found yet. But he hoped to. He hoped to bring them all back here to Ambria by the end of the summer.

He turned and looked through the French doors into her bedroom and saw the huge, soft bed where he'd spent most of the two and a half days when he'd been here before. Memories flooded back. He remembered her and her luscious body and he groaned softly, feeling the surge of desire again.

Pellea was special. He couldn't remember another woman who had ever stuck in his mind the way she did. She'd embedded herself into his heart, his soul, his imagination, and he didn't even want to be free of her. And that was a revelation.

If he survived this summer...

No, he couldn't promise anything, not even to himself. After all, her father was the man who had betrayed his family. He couldn't let himself forget that.

But where was she? She'd been gone a long time. He turned back and looked at the closed doors to her dressing room, then moved to them and called softly, "Pellea."

There was no response.

"Pellea?"

Still nothing. He didn't want to make his call any louder. You never knew who might be at the gate or near enough to it to hear his voice. He tried the knob instead, pushing the door open a bit and calling again, "Pellea?"

There was no answer. It was quite apparent she wasn't there.

CHAPTER THREE

ALARM BELLS RANG IN Monte's head and adrenaline flooded his system. Where had she gone? How had she escaped without him seeing her? What was she doing? Had he overestimated his ability to charm, compared to Leonardo's ability to hand out a power position? Was she a traitor, just like her father?

All that flashed through his mind, sending him reeling. But that only lasted seconds before he'd dismissed it out of hand. She wouldn't do that. There had to be a reason.

The last he'd seen of her she was heading into her large, walk-in closet at the far side of the dressing room. He was there in two strides, and that is when he saw, behind a clothing bar loaded with fluffy gowns, the glimmer of something electronic just beyond a door that had been left slightly ajar.

A secret room behind the clothing storage. Who knew? He certainly hadn't known anything about it when he'd been here before.

Reaching in through the gowns, he pushed the door fully open. And there was Pellea, sitting before a large computer screen that was displaying a number of windows, all showing places in the castle itself. She had a whole command center in here.

"Why you little vixen," he said, astounded. "What do you have here? You've tapped into a gold mine."

She looked up at him, startled, and then resigned.

"I knew I should have closed that door all the way," she muttered to herself.

But he was still captured by the computer screen. "This is the castle security system, isn't it?"

She sighed. "Yes. You caught me."

He shook his head, staring at the screen. "How did you do that?" he asked in wonder.

She shrugged. "My father had this secret room installed years ago. Whenever he wanted to take a look at what was going on, he came to me for a visit. I didn't use it myself at first. I didn't see any need for it. But lately, I've found it quite handy."

"And you can keep things running properly on your own?"

"I've got a certain amount of IT talent. I've read a few books."

He looked at her and smiled. "My admiration grows."

She colored a bit and looked away.

"So you can see what's going on at all the major interior intersections, and a few of the outside venues as well. How convenient." His mind was racing with possibilities.

She pushed away from the desk and sighed again. "Monte, I shouldn't have let you see this."

"You didn't let me. I did it all on my own." He shook his head, still impressed. "Are you going to tell me why?"

She sighed again. "There are times when one might want to do things without being observed. Here in the castle, someone is always watching." She shrugged. "I like a little anonymity in my life. This way I can get a pretty good idea of who is doing what and I can bide my time."

"I see."

She rose and turned toward the door. "And now I really am late." She looked back. He followed her out reluctantly and she closed the door carefully. It seemed to disappear into the background of paneling and molding strips that surrounded it.

"See you later," she said, leading him away from the area. "And stay out of that room."

He frowned as she started off. He didn't want her to leave, and he also didn't want to miss out on anything he didn't have to. On impulse, he called after her, "I want to go with you."

She whirled and stared at him. "What?"

"I'd like to see your father."

She came back towards him, shocked and looking for a way to refuse. "But you can't. He's bedridden. He's in no condition…"

"I won't show myself to him. I won't hurt him." He shook his head and frowned. "But, Pellea, he's one of the few remaining ties to my parents left alive. He's from their generation. He knew them, worked with them. He was close to them at one time." He shrugged, looking oddly vulnerable in his emotional reactions. "I just want to see him, hear his voice. I promise I won't do anything to jeopardize his health—or even his emotional well-being in any way."

She studied him and wondered what she really knew about him. The way he felt about her father had been clear almost from the first. He was wrong about her father. She'd spent a lot of time agonizing over that, wondering how she could make him understand that her father was just a part of his time and place, that he had only done what he had to do, that he was really a man of great compassion and honesty. Maybe this would be a chance to do just that.

"You won't confront him about anything?"

"No. I swear." He half smiled. "I swear on my parents' memories. Do you trust me?"

She groaned. "God help me, I do." She searched his eyes. "All right. But you'll have to be careful. If you're caught, I'll claim you forced me to take you with me."

He smiled at her sideways, knowing she was lying. If he were caught, she would do her best to free him. She talked a good game, but deep down, she had a lot of integrity. And she was at least half in love with him. That gave him a twinge. More the fool was she.

"I only go when no one else is there," she was telling him. "I know when the nurse goes on her break and how long she takes."

He nodded. He'd always known she was quick and

sure at everything she did. He would have expected as much from her.

"Keep your eyes downcast," she lectured as they prepared to head into the hallway. "I try to go at a quiet time of day, but there might be someone in the halls. Don't make eye contact with anyone or you'll surely blow your cover. You can't help but look regal, can you? Take smaller steps. Try to slump your shoulders a little. A little more." She made a face. "Here." She whacked one shoulder to make it droop, and then the other, a tiny smile on her lips. "That's better," she said with satisfaction.

He was suspicious. She hadn't held back much. "You enjoyed that, didn't you?"

"Giving you a whack?" She allowed herself a tight smile. "Certainly not. I don't believe in corporal punishment."

"Liar." He was laughing at her. "Are you going to try to convince me that it hurt you more than it hurt me?"

She didn't bother to respond. Giving him a look, she stepped out into the hallway, wondering if she was crazy to do this. But she was being honest when she said she trusted him to come along and see her father with her. Was she letting her heart rule her head? Probably. But she'd made her decision and she would stick to it.

Still, that didn't mean she was sanguine about it all. Why had he come back? Why now, just when she had everything set the way it had to be?

And why was her heart beating like a caged bird inside her chest? It didn't matter that she loved him. She couldn't ever be with him again. She had a baby to think about. And no time to indulge in emotions. Taking Monte with her was a risk, but she didn't really have a lot of choice—unless she wanted to turn him in to the guard.

She thought about doing exactly that for a few seconds, a smile playing on her lips. That would take them back full circle, wouldn't it? But it wasn't going to happen.

Don't worry, sweet baby, she said silently to her child. *I won't let anything hurt your father.* She said a tiny prayer and added, *I hope.*

Monte wasn't often haunted by self-doubt. In fact, his opinions and decisions were usually rock-solid. Once made, no wavering. But watching Pellea with her father gave him a sense that the earth might not be quite as firm under his feet as he'd assumed.

In the first place, he wasn't really sure why she'd let him come with her. She knew how the need for retribution burned in him and yet she'd let him come here where he would have a full view of the man, his enemy, lying there, helpless. Didn't she know how dangerous that was?

It would be easy to harm the old man. He was still handsome in an aged, fragile way, like a relic of past power. His face was drawn and lined, his color pale, his thin hair silver. Blue veins stood out in his slender hands. He was so vulnerable, so completely defenseless. Someone who moved on pure gut reaction would have done him in by now. Luckily, that wasn't Monte's style.

He would never do such a thing, but she didn't really know that. She'd taken a risk. But for what?

He watched as the object of his long, deep hatred struggled to talk to the daughter he obviously loved more than life itself, and he found his emotions tangling a bit. Could he really feel pity for a man who had helped ruin his family?

No. That couldn't happen.

Still, an element confused the issue. And to be this close to someone who had lived with and worked with his parents gave him a special sense of his own history. He couldn't deny that.

And there was something else, a certain primal longing that he couldn't control. He'd had it ever since that day twenty-five years ago when he'd been rushed out of the burning castle, and he had forever lost his parents. He'd grown up with all the privileges of his class: the schools, the high life, the international relationships. But he would have thrown it all out if that could have bought him a real, loving family—the kind you saw in movies, the kind you dreamed about in the middle of the night. Instead, he had this empty ache in his heart.

And that made watching Pellea and her father all the more effective. From his position in the entryway, he could see her bending lovingly over her father and dropping a kiss on his forehead. She talked softly to him, wiping his forehead with a cool, damp cloth, straightening his covers, plumping his pillow. The love she had for the man radiated from her every move. And he felt very similarly. She was obviously a brilliant bit of sun in his rather dark life.

"How are you feeling?" she asked.

"Much better now that you're here, my dear."

"I'm only here for a moment. I must get back. The masked ball is tonight."

"Ah, yes." He took hold of her hand. "So tonight you and Leonardo will announce your engagement?"

"Yes. Leonardo is prepared."

"What a relief to have this coming so quickly. To be able to see you protected before I go…"

"Don't talk about going."

"We all have to do it, my dear. My time has come."

Pellea made a dove-like noise and bent down to kiss his cheek. "No. You just need to get out more. See some people." Rising a bit, she had a thought. "I know. I'll have the nurse bring you to the ball so that you can see for yourself…."

"Hush, Pellea," he said, shaking his head. "I'm not going anywhere. I'm comfortable here and I'm too weak to leave this bed."

Reluctantly, she nodded. She'd known he would say that, but she'd hoped he might change his mind and try to take a step back into the world. A deep, abiding sadness settled into her soul as she faced the fact that he wasn't even tempted to try. He was preparing for the end, and nothing she said or did would change that. Tears threatened and she forced them back. She would have to save her grieving for another time.

Right now, she had another goal in mind. She was

hoping to prove something to Monte, and she was gambling that her father would respond in the tone and tenor that she'd heard from him so often before. If he went in a different direction, there was no telling what might happen. Glancing back at where Monte stood in the shadows, she made her decision. She was going to risk it—her leap of faith.

"Father, do you ever think of the past? About how we got here and why we are the way we are?"

He coughed and nodded. "I think of very little else these days."

"Do you think about the night the castle burned?"

"That was before you were born."

"Yes. But I feel as though that night molded my life in many ways."

He grasped her hand as though to make her stop it. "But why? It had nothing to do with you."

"But it was such a terrible way to start a new regime, the regime I've lived under all my life."

"Ugly things always happen in war." He turned his face away as though he didn't want to talk about it. "These things can't be helped."

She could feel Monte's anger beginning to simmer even though she didn't look at him. She hesitated. If her father wasn't going to express his remorse, she might only be doing damage by making him talk. Could Monte control his emotions? Was it worth it to push this further?

She had to try. She leaned forward.

"But, Father, you always say so many mistakes were made."

"Mistakes are human. That is just the way it is."

Monte made a sound that was very close to a growl. She shook her head, still unwilling to look his way, but ready to give up. What she'd hoped for just wasn't going to happen.

"All right, Father," she began, straightening and preparing to get Monte out of here before he did something ugly.

But suddenly her father was speaking again. "The burning of the castle was a terrible thing," he was saying, though he was speaking so softly she wondered if Monte could hear him. "And the assassination of the king and queen was even worse."

Relief bloomed in her chest. "What happened?" she prompted him. "How did it get so out of control?"

"You can go into a war with all sorts of lofty ambitions, but once the fuse is lit, the fire can be uncontrollable. It wasn't supposed to happen that way. Many of us were sick at heart for years afterwards. I still think of it with pain and deep, deep regret."

This was more like it. She only hoped Monte could hear it and that he was taking it as a sincere recollection, not a rationalization. She laced her fingers with her father's long, trembling ones.

"Tell me again, why did you sign on with the rebels?"

"I was very callow and I felt the DeAngelis family had grown arrogant with too much power. They were rejecting all forms of modernization. Something was needed to shake the country up. We were impatient. We thought something had to be done."

"And now?"

"Now I think that we should have moved more slowly, attempted dialogue instead of attack."

"So you regret how things developed?"

"I regret it deeply."

She glanced back at Monte. His face looked like a storm cloud. Wasn't he getting it? Didn't he see how her father had suffered as well? Maybe not. Maybe she was tilting at windmills. She turned back to her father and asked a question for herself.

"Then why do you want me to marry Leonardo and just perpetuate this regime?"

Her father coughed again and held a handkerchief to his lips. "He'll be better than his father. He has some good ideas. And your influence on him will work wonders." He managed a weak smile for his beloved daughter. "Once you are married to Leonardo, it will be much more difficult for anyone to hurt you."

She smiled down at him and blotted his forehead with the damp cloth. He wouldn't be so sure of that if he knew that at this very moment, danger lurked around her on all sides. Better he should never know that she was carrying Monte's child.

"I must go, Father. I've got to prepare for the ball."

"Yes. Go, my darling. Have a wonderful time."

"I'll be back in the morning to tell you all about it," she promised as she rose from his side.

She hurried toward the door, jerking her head at Monte to follow. She didn't like the look on his face. It seemed his hatred for her father was too strong for him to see what a dear and wonderful man he really was. Well, so be it. She'd done her best to show him the truth. You could lead a horse to water and all that.

But they were late. She had a path laid out and a routine, and now she knew she was venturing out into the unknown. At her usual time, she never met anyone in the halls. Now—who knew?

"We have to hurry," she said once they were outside the room. She quickly looked up and down the empty hallway. "I've got to meet Leonardo in just a short time." She started off. "Quickly. We don't want to meet anyone if we can help it."

The words were barely out of her mouth when she heard loud footsteps coming from around the bend in the walkway. Only boots could make such a racket. It had to be the guards. It sounded like two of them.

"Quick," she said, reaching for the closest door. "In here."

Though she knew the castle well, she wasn't sure what door she'd reached for. There was a library along this corridor, and a few bedrooms of lower-ranking relatives of the Granvillis. Any one of them could have yielded disaster. But for once, she was in luck. The door she'd chosen opened to reveal a very small broom closet.

Monte looked in and didn't see room for them both. He turned back to tell her, but she wasn't listening.

"In," she whispered urgently, and gave him a shove,

then came pushing in behind him, closing the door as quietly as she could. But was it quietly enough? Pressed close together, they each held their breath, listening as the boots came closer. And closer. And then stopped, right outside the door.

Pellea looked up at Monte, her eyes huge and anxious. He looked down at her and smiled. It was dark in the closet, but enough light came in around the door to let him make out her features. She was so beautiful and so close against him. He wanted to kiss her. But more important things had cropped up. So he reached around her and took hold of the knob from the inside.

There was a muttering conversation they couldn't make out, and then one of the guards tried the knob. Monte clamped down on his lower lip, holding the knob with all his might.

"It's locked," one of the guards said. "We'll have to find the concierge and get a key."

The other guard swore, but they began to drift off, walking slowly this time and chattering among themselves.

Monte relaxed and let go of the knob, letting out a long sigh of relief. When he looked down, she was smiling up at him, and this time he kissed her.

He'd been thinking about this kiss for so long, and now, finally, here it was. Her lips were smooth as silk, warm and inviting, and for just a moment, she opened enough to let his tongue flicker into the heat she held deeper. Then she tried to pull away, but he took her head in his hands and kissed her longer, deeper, and he felt her begin to melt in his arms.

Her body was molded to his and he could feel her heart begin to pound again, just as it had when they'd almost been caught. The excitement lit a flame in him and he pulled her closer, kissed her harder, wanted her all to himself, body and soul.

It was as though he'd forgotten where they were, what was happening around them. But Pellea hadn't.

"Monte," she finally managed to gasp, pushing him as hard as she could. "We have to go while we have the chance!"

He knew she was right and he let her pull away, but reluctantly. Still, he'd found out what he needed to know. The magic still lived between them and they could turn it on effortlessly. And, he hoped, a bit later, they would.

But now she opened the door tentatively and looked out. There was no one in the hall. She slipped out and he followed and they hurried to her gate, alert for any hint of anyone else coming their way. But they were lucky. She used a remote to open the gate as they approached. In seconds, they were safely inside.

The moment the gate closed, Monte turned and tried to take her into his arms again, but she backed away, trying hard to glare at him.

"Just stop it," she told him.

But he was shaking his head. "You can't marry Leonardo. Not when you can kiss me like that."

She stared at him for a moment. How could she have let this happen? He knew, he could tell that she was so in love with him, she could hardly contain it. She could protest all she wanted, he wasn't going to believe her. If she wasn't very careful, he would realize the precious secret that she was keeping from him, and if that happened, they would both be in terrible trouble.

Feeling overwhelmed, she groaned, her head in her hands. "Why are you torturing me like this?"

He put a finger under her chin and forced her head up to meet his gaze. "Maybe a little torture will make you see the light."

"There's no light," she said sadly, her eyes huge with tragedy. "There's only darkness."

He'd been about to try to kiss her again, but something in her tone stopped him and he hesitated. Just a few weeks before, their relationship had been light and exciting, a romp despite the dangers they faced. They had made love, but they had also laughed a lot, and teased and played and generally enjoyed each other. Something had changed since then. Was it doubt? Wariness? Or fear?

He wasn't sure, but it bothered him and it held him off long enough for her to pivot out of his control.

"Gotta go," she said as she started for the gate, prepared to dash off again.

He took a step after her. "You're not planning to tell Leonardo I'm here, are you?" he said. His tone was teasing, as though he was confident she had no such plans.

She turned and looked at him, tempted to do or say something that would shake that annoying surety he had.

But she resisted that temptation. Instead, she told the truth.

"I'm hoping you won't be here any longer by the time I get back."

He appeared surprised. "Where would I go?"

She shook her head. It was obviously no use to try, but she had to make her case quickly and clearly. "Please, Monte," she said earnestly. "Go back the way you came in. Just do this for me. It will make my life a whole lot easier."

"Pellea, this is not your problem. I'll handle it."

She half laughed at his confidence. "What do you mean, not my problem? That's exactly what you are. My problem."

"Relax," he advised. "I'm just going to work on my objective."

"Which is?"

"I told you. I'm here to kidnap you and take you back to the continent with me."

"Oh, get off it. You can't kidnap me. I'm guarded day and night."

"Really? Well, where were your wonderful guards when I found my way into your chambers?"

She didn't have an answer for that one so she changed the subject. "What's the point? Why would you kidnap me?"

He shrugged. "To show them I can."

She threw up her hands. "Oh, brother."

"I want to show the Granvillis that I've been here and taken something precious to them."

Her eyes widened. "You think I'm precious?"

His smile was almost too personal. "I know you are. You're their most beautiful, desirable woman."

That gave her pause. Was she supposed to feel flattered by that? Well, she sort of did, but she wouldn't admit it.

"Gee, thanks. You make me feel like a prize horse." She shook her head. "So to you, this is just part of some war game?"

The laughter left his gaze. "Oh, no. This is no game. This is deadly serious."

There was something chilling in the way he said that. She shivered and tried to pretend she hadn't.

"So you grab me. You throw me over your shoulder and carry me back to your cave. You go 'nah nah nah' to the powers that be in Ambria." She shrugged. "What does that gain you?"

He watched her steadily, making her wonder what he saw. "The purpose is not just to thumb my nose at the Granvillis. The purpose is to cast them into disarray, to make them feel vulnerable and stupid. To throw them off their game. Let them spend their time obsessing on how I could have possibly gotten into the castle, how I could have possibly taken you out without someone seeing. Let them worry. It will make them weaker."

"You're crazy," she said for lack of anything else to say. And he was crazy if he thought the Granvillis would tumble into ruin because of a kidnapping or two.

"I'd like to see them tightening their defenses all around," he went on, "and begin scurrying about, looking for the chinks in their armor. There are people here who watch what they do and report to us. This will give us a better idea of where the weak spots are."

She nodded. She understood the theory behind all this. But it didn't make her any happier with it.

"So when you get right down to it, it doesn't have to be me," she noted. "You could take back something else of importance. The tiara, for instance."

Something moved behind his eyes, but he only smiled. "I'd rather take you."

"Well, you're not going to. So why not just get out of my hair and go back where you came from?"

He shook his head slowly, his blue eyes dark with shadows. "Sorry, Pellea. I've got things I must do here."

She sighed. She knew exactly what he would be doing while she was gone. He would be in her secret room, checking out what was going on all over the castle. Making his plans. Ruining her life. A wave of despair flooded through her. What had she done? Why hadn't she been more careful?

"Arrgghh!" she said, making a small wail of agony.

But right now she couldn't think about that. She had to go meet Leonardo or he would show up here.

"You stay out of my closet room," she told him with a warning look, knowing he wouldn't listen to a word she said. "Okay?" She glared at him, not bothering to wait for an answer. "I'll be back quicker than you think."

He laughed, watching her go, enjoying the way her

hips swayed in time with her gorgeous hair. And then she was gone and he headed straight for the closet.

To the casual eye, there was nothing of note to suggest a door to another room. The wall seemed solid enough. He tried to remember what she'd done to close it, but he hadn't been paying attention at the time. There had to be something—a special knock or a latch or a pressure point. He banged and pushed and tried to slide things, but nothing gave way.

"If this needs a magic password, I'm out of luck," he muttered to himself as he made his various attempts.

He kicked a little side panel, more in frustration than hope, and the door began to creak open. "It's always the ones you don't suspect," he said, laughing.

The small room inside was unprepossessing, having space only for a computer and a small table. And there on the screen was access to views of practically every public area, all over the castle. A secret room with centralized power no one else knew about. Ingenious.

Still, someone had built it. Someone had wired it. Someone had to know electronics were constantly running in here. The use of electricity alone would tip off the suspicious. So someone in the workings of the place was on her side.

But what was "her side" exactly? That was something he still had to find out.

The sound of Pellea's entry gong made him jerk. He lifted his head and listened. A woman's voice seemed to be calling out, and then, a moment later, singing. She'd obviously come into the courtyard.

Moving silently, he made his way out of the secret room, closing the door firmly. He moved carefully into the dressing area, planning to use the high wardrobe as a shield as he had done earlier, in order to see who it was without being seen. As he came out of the closet and made his way to slip behind the tall piece of furniture, a pretty, pleasantly rounded young woman stepped into the room, catching sight of him just before he found his hiding place.

She gasped. Their gazes met. Her mouth opened. He reached out to stop her, but he was too late.

She screamed at the top of her lungs.

CHAPTER FOUR

MONTE MOVED LIKE LIGHTNING but it felt like slow motion to him. In no time his hand was over the intruder's mouth and he was pulling her roughly into the room and kicking the French door closed with such a snap, he was afraid for a moment that the glass would crack.

Pulling her tightly against his chest, he snarled in her ear, "Shut the hell up and do it now."

She pulled her breath into her lungs in hysterical gasps, and he yanked her more tightly.

"Now!" he demanded.

She closed her eyes and tried very hard. He could feel the effort she put into it, and he began to relax. They waited, counting off the seconds, to see if anyone had heard the scream and was coming to the rescue. Nothing seemed to stir. At last, he decided the time for alarm was over and he began to release her slowly, ready to reassert control if she tried to scream again.

"Okay," he whispered close to her ear. "I'm going to let go now. If you make a sound, I'll have to knock you flat."

She nodded, accepting his terms. But she didn't seem

to have any intention of a repeat. As he freed her, she turned, her gaze sweeping over him in wonder.

"Wait," she said, eyes like saucers. "I've seen you before. You were here a couple of months ago."

By now, he'd recognized her as well. She was Pellea's favorite maid. He hadn't interacted with her when he'd been here before, but he'd seen her when she'd dropped by to deal with some things Pellea needed done. Pellea had trusted her to keep his presence a secret then. He only hoped that trust was warranted—and could hold for now.

But signs were good. He liked the sparkle in her eyes. He gave her a lopsided smile. "I'm back."

"So I see." She cocked her head to the side, looking him over, then narrowing her gaze. "And is my mistress happy that you're here?"

He shrugged. "Hard to tell. But she didn't throw anything at me."

Her smile was open-hearted. "That's a good sign."

He drew in a deep breath, feeling better about the situation. "What's your name?" he asked.

"Pellea calls me Kimmee."

"Then I shall do the same." He didn't offer his own name and wondered if she knew who he was. He doubted it. Pellea wouldn't be that reckless, would she?

"I've been here for a couple of hours now," he told her. "Pellea has seen me. We've been chatting, going over old times."

Kimmee grinned. "Delightful."

He smiled back, but added a warning look. "I'm

sure you don't talk about your mistress's assignations to others."

"Of course not," she said brightly. "I only wish she had a few."

He blinked. "What do you mean?"

She shrugged, giving him a sly look. "You're the only one I know of."

He laughed. She had said the one thing that would warm his heart and she probably knew it, but it made him happy anyway.

"You're not trying to tell me your mistress has no suitors, are you?" he teased skeptically.

"Oh, no, of course not. But she generally scorns them all."

He looked at her levelly. "Even Leonardo?" he asked.

She hesitated, obviously reluctant to give her candid opinion on that score. He let her off the hook with a shrug.

"Never mind. I know she's promised to him at this point." He cocked an eyebrow. "I just don't accept it."

She nodded. "Good," she whispered softly, then shook her head as though wishing she hadn't spoken. Turning away, she reached for the ball gown hanging in front of the wardrobe. "I just came by to check that the gown was properly hung and wrinkle-free," she said, smoothing the skirt a bit. "Isn't it gorgeous?"

"Yes, it is."

"I can't wait to see her dancing in this," Kimmee added.

"Neither can I," he murmured, and at the same time, an idea came to him. He frowned, wondering if he should trust thoughts spurred on by his overwhelming desire for all things Pellea. It was a crazy idea, but the more he mulled it over, the more he realized it could serve more than one purpose and fit into much of what he hoped to accomplish. So why not give it a try?

He studied the pretty maid for a moment, trying to evaluate just how much he dared depend on her. Her eyes sparkled in a way that made him wonder how a fun-loving girl like this would keep such a secret. He knew he had better be prepared to deal with the fallout, should there be any. After all, he didn't have much choice. Either he would tie her up and gag her and throw her into a closet, or he would appeal to her better nature.

"Tell me, Kimmee, do you love your mistress?"

"Oh, yes." Kimmee smiled. "She's my best friend. We've been mates since we were five years old."

He nodded, frowning thoughtfully. "Then you'll keep a secret," he said. "A secret that could get me killed if you reveal it."

Her eyes widened and she went very still. "Of course."

His own gaze was hard and assessing as he pinned her with it. "You swear on your honor?"

She shook her head, looking completely earnest. "I swear on my honor. I swear on my life. I swear on my…"

He held a hand up. "I get the idea, Kimmee. You really mean it. So I'm going to trust you."

She waited, wide-eyed.

He looked into her face, his own deadly serious.

"I want to go to the ball."

"Oh, sir!" She threw her hands up to her mouth. "Oh, my goodness! Where? How?"

"That's where you come in. Find me a costume and a nice, secure mask." He cocked an eyebrow and smiled at her. "Can you do that?"

"Impossible," she cried. "Simply impossible." But a smile was beginning to tease the corners of her mouth. "Well, maybe." She thought a moment longer, then smiled impishly. "It would be fun, wouldn't it?"

He grinned at her.

"Will you want a sword?" she asked, her enthusiasm growing by leaps and bounds.

He grimaced. "I think not. It might be too tempting to use it on Leonardo."

"I know what you mean," she said, nodding wisely.

He got a real kick out of her. She was so ready to join in on his plans and at the same time, she seemed to be thoroughly loyal to the mistress she considered her best friend. It was a helpful combination to work with.

He lifted his head, looking at the ball gown and thinking of how it would look with his favorite woman filling it out in all the right places. "All I want to do is go to the ball and dance with Pellea."

"How romantic," Kimmee said, sighing. Then her gaze sharpened as she realized what he might be describing. "You mean…?"

"Yes." He nodded. "Secretly. I want to surprise Pellea."

Kimmee gave a bubbling laugh, obviously delighted with the concept. "I think Leonardo will be even more surprised."

He shook his head and gave her a warning look. "That is something I'll have to guard against."

She sighed. "I understand. But it would be fun to see his face."

He frowned, wondering if he was letting her get a little too much into this.

"See what you can do," he said. "But don't forget. If Leonardo finds out…" He drew his finger across his throat like a knife and made a cutting sound. "I'll be dead and Pellea will be in big trouble."

She shook her head, eyes wide and sincere. "You can count on me, sir. And as for the costume…" She put her hand over her heart. "I'll do my best."

Pellea returned a half hour later, bristling with determination.

"I've brought you something to eat," she said, handing him a neatly wrapped, grilled chicken leg and a small loaf of artisan bread. He was sitting at a small table near her fountain, looking for all the world like a Parisian playboy at a sidewalk café. "And I've brought you news."

"News, huh? Let me guess." He put his hand to his forehead as though taking transmissions from space.

"Leonardo has decided to join the national ballet and forget all about this crazy marriage stuff. Am I right?"

She glared at him. "I'm warning you, don't take the man lightly."

"Oh, I don't. Believe me." He began to unwrap the chicken leg. He hadn't eaten for hours and he was more than ready to partake of what she'd brought him. "So what is the news?"

"Leonardo talked to his father and we've decided to move the wedding up." Her chin rose defiantly. "We're getting married in two days."

He put down the chicken leg, hunger forgotten, and stared at her with eyes that had turned icy silver. "What's the rush?" he asked with deceptive calm.

The look in his gaze made her nervous. He seemed utterly peaceful, and yet there was a sense in the air that a keg of dynamite was about to blow.

She turned away, pacing, thinking about how nice and simple life had been before she'd found him lurking in her garden that day. Her path had been relatively clear at the time. True, she had been fighting her father over his wish that she marry Leonardo. But that was relatively easy to deal with compared to what she had now.

The irony was that her father would get his wish, and she'd done it to herself. She would marry Leonardo. She would be the first lady of the land and just about impervious to attack. Just as her father so obsessively craved, she would be as safe as she could possibly be.

But even that wasn't perfect safety. There were a thousand chinks in her armor and the path ahead was perilous. Everything she did, every decision she made, could have unforeseen repercussions. She had set a course and now the winds would take her to her destination. Was it the best destination for her or was it a mirage? Was she right or was she wrong? If only she knew.

Looking out into the courtyard, Pellea shivered with a premonition of what might be to come.

Monte watched her from under lowered brows, munching on a bite of chicken. Much as she was trying to hide it, he could see that she was in a special sort of agony and he couldn't for the life of him understand why. What was her hurry to marry Leonardo? What made her so anxious to cement those ties?

Motivations were often difficult to untangle and understand. What were hers? Did it really mean everything to her to have her father satisfied that she was safe, and to do it before it was too late? Evidence did suggest that he was fading fast. Was that what moved her? He couldn't think what else it could be. But was that really enough to make her rush to Leonardo's arms? Or was there something going on that he didn't know about?

"I suppose the powers that be are in favor of this wedding?" he mentioned casually.

She nodded. "Believe me, everything around here is planned to the nth degree. Public-relations values hold sway over everything."

"I've noticed. That's what makes me wonder. What's the deal with this wedding coming on so suddenly? I would think the regime would try to milk all the publicity they could possibly get out of a long engagement."

"Interesting theory," she said softly, pretending to be busy folding clothes away.

"Why?" he asked bluntly. "Why so soon?"

"You'd have to ask Leonardo about that," she said evasively.

"Maybe I will. If I get the chance." He looked at her sharply, trying to read her mind. "I can't help but think he has a plan in mind. There has to be a reason."

"Sometimes people just want to do things quickly," she said, getting annoyed with his persistence.

"Um-hmm." He didn't buy that for a minute. The more he let the idea of such a marriage—the ultimate marriage of convenience—linger in his mind, the more he hated it. Pellea couldn't be with Leonardo. Everything in him rebelled at the thought.

Pellea belonged to him.

That was nonsense, of course. How could she be his when he wouldn't do what needed to be done to take that responsibility in hand himself? After all, he'd refused to step up and do the things a man did when making a woman his own. As his old tutor might say, he craved the honey but refused to tend to the bees.

Still in some deep, gut-level part of him, she was his and had been since the moment he'd first laid eyes on her. He'd put his stamp on her, his brand, his seal. He'd held her and loved her, body and soul, and he wanted her available for more of the same. She was his, damn it!

But what was he prepared to do about it?

That was the question.

He watched her, taking in the grace and loveliness of her form and movement, the full, luscious temptation of her exciting body, the beauty of her perfect face, and the question burned inside him. What was he prepared to do? It was working into a drumbeat in his head and in his heart. What? Just exactly what?

"You don't love him."

The words came out loud and clear and yet he was surprised when he said them. He hadn't planned to say anything of the sort. Still, once it was out, he was glad he'd said it. The truth was out now, like a flag, a banner, a warning that couldn't be ignored any longer. And why not? Truth was supposed to set you free.

And she didn't love Leonardo. It was obvious in the way she talked to him and talked about him. She was using him and he was using her. They had practically said as much in front of him—though neither had known it at the time. Why not leave it out there in the open where it could be dealt with?

"You don't love him," he said again, even more firmly this time.

She whirled to face him, her arms folded, her eyes flashing. "How do you know?" she challenged, her chin high.

A slow smile began to curl his lips. As long as they were speaking truth, why not add a bit more?

"I know, Pellea. I know very well. Because…" He paused, not really for dramatic effect, although that was what he ended up with. He paused because for just a second, he wondered if he really dared say this.

"Because you love me," he said at last.

The shock of his words seemed to crackle in the air.

She gasped. "Oh! Of all the…" Her cheeks turned bright red and she choked and had to cough for a moment. "I never told you that!"

He sat back and surveyed her levelly. "You didn't have to tell me with words. Your body told me all I would ever need to know." His gaze skimmed over her creamy skin. "Every time I touch you your body resonates like a fine instrument. You were born to play to my tune."

She stood staring at him, shaking her head as though she couldn't believe anyone would have the gall to say such things. "Of all the egos in the world…"

"Mine's the best?" he prompted, then shrugged with a lopsided grin. "Of course."

She held her breath and counted to ten, not really sure if she was trying to hold back anger or a smile. He did appear ridiculously adorable sitting there looking pleased with himself. She let her breath back out and tried for logic and reason. It would obviously be best to leave flights of fancy and leaps of faith behind.

"I don't love you," she lied with all her heart. Tears suddenly threatened, but she wouldn't allow them. Not now. "I can't love you. Don't you see that? Don't ever say that to me again."

Something in her voice reached in and made a grab for his heartstrings. Had he actually hurt her with his careless words? That was the last thing he would ever want to do.

"Pellea." He rose and reached for her.

She tried to turn away but he wouldn't let her. His arms came around her, holding her close against his chest, and he stroked her hair.

"Pellea, darling…"

She lifted her face, her lips trembling. He looked down and melted. No woman had ever been softer in his arms. Instantly, his mouth was on hers, touching, testing, probing, lighting her pulse on fire. She kissed him in return for as long as she dared, then pulled back, though she was still in the circle of his embrace. She tried to frown.

"You taste like chicken," she said, blinking up at him.

He smiled, and a warm sense of his affection for her was plain to see. "You taste like heaven," he countered.

She closed her eyes and shook her head. "Oh, please, Monte. Let me go."

He did so reluctantly, and she drew back slowly, looking toward him with large, sad eyes and thinking, *If only…*

He watched her, feeling strangely helpless, though he wasn't really sure why. With a sigh, she turned and went back to pacing.

"We have to get you out of here," she fretted while he sat down again and leaned back in his chair. "If I can get you out of the castle, do you have a way to get back to the continent?"

He waved away the very concept. "I'm not going anywhere," he said confidently. "And when I do go, I'll take care of myself. I've got resources. No need to worry about me."

She stopped, shaking her head as she looked at him. How could she not worry about him? That was pretty much all she was thinking about right now. She needed him to leave before he found out about the baby. And even more important, she wanted him to go because she wanted him to stay alive. But there was no point in bringing that up. He would only laugh at the danger. Still, she had to try to get him to see reason.

"There is more news," she told him, leaning against the opposite chair. "Rumors are flying."

He paused, the chicken leg halfway to his mouth. He put it down again and gazed at her. "What kind of rumors?"

She turned and sank into the chair she'd been leaning on. "There's talk of a force preparing for an Ambrian invasion."

He raised one sleek eyebrow and looked amused. "By whom?"

"Ex-Ambrians, naturally. Trying to take the country back."

His sharp, all-knowing gaze seemed to see right into her soul as he leaned closer across the table. "And you believe that?"

"Are you kidding?" She threw her hands up. "I can see it with my own eyes. What else are you doing here?"

He gave her another view of his slow, sexy smile. "I came to kidnap you, not to start a revolution. I thought I'd made that perfectly clear."

She leaned forward, searching his eyes. "So it's true. You are planning to take over this country."

He shrugged, all careless confidence. "Someday, sure." His smile was especially knowing and provocative. "Not this weekend though. I've got other plans."

He had other plans. Well, wasn't that just dandy? He had plans and she had issues of life and death to contend with. She wanted to strangle him. Or at least make him wince a little. She rose, towering over him and pointing toward her gateway.

"You've got to go. Now!"

He looked surprised at her vehemence, and then as though his feelings were hurt, he said, "I'm eating."

"You can take the food with you."

He frowned. "But I'm almost done." He took another bite. "This is actually pretty good chicken."

She stared at him, at her wit's end, then sank slowly back into the chair, her head in her hands. What could she do? She couldn't scream for help. That could get him killed. She couldn't pick him up and carry him to the doorway. That would get *her* killed. Or at least badly injured. She was stuck here in her chambers, stuck with the man she loved, the father of her child, the man whose kisses sent her into orbit every time, and everything depended on getting rid of him somehow. What on earth was she going to do?

"I hate you," she said, though it was more of a moan than a sentence.

"Good," he responded. "I like a woman with passion."

She rolled her eyes. Why couldn't he ever be serious? It was maddening. "My hatred would be more effective if I had a dagger instead," she commented dryly.

He waved a finger at her. "No threats. There's nothing quite so deadly to a good relationship. Don't go down that road."

She pouted, feeling grumpy and as though she wasn't being taken seriously. "Who said we had a good relationship?"

He looked surprised. "Don't we?" Reaching out, he took her hand. "It's certainly the best I've ever had," he said softly, his eyes glowing with the sort of affection that made her breath catch in her throat.

She curled her fingers around his. She couldn't help it. She did love him so.

She wasn't sure why. He had done little so far other than make her life more difficult. He hadn't promised her anything but kisses and lovemaking. Was that enough to give your heart for?

Hardly. Pellea was a student of history and she knew very well that people living on love tended to starve pretty quickly. What began with excitement and promises usually ended in bleak prospects and recriminations.

The gong sounded, making her jump. She pulled away

her hand and looked at him. He shrugged as though he regretted the interruption.

"I'll take my food into the library," he offered. "Just don't forget and bring your guest in there."

"I won't," she said back softly, watching him go and then hurrying to the entryway.

It was Magda, her hairdresser, making plans for their session. The older woman was dressed like a gypsy with scarves and belts everywhere. She was a bit of a character, but she had a definite talent with hair.

"I'll be back in half an hour," she warned. "You be ready. I'm going to need extra time to weave your hair around the tiara. It's not what I usually do, you know."

"Yes, I know, Magda," Pellea said, smiling. "And I appreciate that you are willing to give it a try. I'm sure we'll work something out together."

Magda grumbled a bit, but she seemed to be looking forward to the challenge. "Half an hour," she warned again as she started off toward the supply room to prepare for the session.

Pellea had just begun to close the gate when Kimmee came breezing around the corner.

"Hi," she called, rushing forward. "Don't close me out."

Pellea gave her a welcoming smile but didn't encourage her to come into the courtyard. "I'm in a bit of a hurry tonight," she warned her. "I've got the hairdresser coming and…"

"I just need to give your gown a last-minute check

for wrinkles," Kimmee said cheerfully, ignoring Pellea's obvious hint and coming right on in.

"Where is he?" she whispered, eyes sparkling, as she squeezed past.

"Who?" Pellea responded, startled.

Kimmee grinned. "I saw him when I was here earlier. You were out, but he was here." She winked. "I said hello." She looked around, merrily furtive. "We spoke."

"Oh."

Pellea swallowed hard with regret. This was not good. This was exactly what she'd hoped to avoid. Kimmee had kept the secret before, but would she again?

"He is so gorgeous," Kimmee whispered happily. "I'm so glad for you. You needed someone gorgeous in your life."

Pellea shook her head, worried and not sure how to deal with this. "But, Kimmee, it's not like that. You know I'm going to marry Leonardo and..."

"All the more reason you need a gorgeous man. No one said it had to be a forever man." Her smile was impish. "Just take some happiness where you can. You deserve it."

She looked at her maid in despair. It was all very well for her to be giving shallow comfort for activities that were clearly not in good taste. But here she was, hoisted on her own petard, as it were—taking advice that could ruin her life. But what was she going to do—beg a servant not to gossip? Might as well ask a bird not to fly.

Of course, Kimmee was more than a mere servant.

In many ways, she had always been her best friend. That might make a difference. It had in the past. But not being sure was nerve-wracking. After all, this was pretty much a life-or-death situation.

She closed her eyes and said a little prayer. "Kimmee," she began nervously.

"Don't worry, Pel," Kimmee said softly. She reached out and touched her mistress's arm, her eyes warm with an abiding affection. She'd used the name she'd called Pellea when they were young playmates. "I'm just happy that…" She shrugged, but they both knew what she was talking about. "I'd never, ever tell anyone else. It's just you and me."

Tears filled Pellea's eyes. "Thank you," she whispered.

Kimmee kissed Pellea's cheek, as though on impulse and nodded. Then suddenly, as she noticed Monte coming into the doorway to the library, she was the dutiful servant once again. "Oh, miss, let me take a look at that gown."

Monte leaned against the doorjamb, his shirt open, his hair mussed, looking for all the world like an incredibly handsome buccaneer.

"Hey, Kimmee," he said.

"Hello, sir." She waved, then had second thoughts and curtsied. As she rose from her deep bow, Pellea was behind her and Kimmee risked an A-OK wink to show him plans were afoot and all was going swimmingly. "I hope things are going well with you," she added politely.

"Absolutely," he told her. "I've just had a nice little meal and I'm feeling pretty chipper."

She laughed and turned back to her work, completed it quickly, and turned to go.

"Well, miss, I just wanted to check on the gown and remind you I'll be here to help you get into it in about an hour. Will that suit?"

"That will suit. Magda should be through by then." She smiled at the young woman. "Thank you, Kimmee," she said, giving her a hug as she passed. "I hope you know how much I appreciate you."

"Of course, miss. My only wish is for your happiness. You should know that by now."

"I do. You're a treasure."

The maid waved at them both. "I'll be back in a bit. See you."

"Goodbye, Kimmee," Monte said, retreating into the library again.

But Pellea watched her go, deep in thought. In a few hours, she would be at the ball, dancing with Leonardo and preparing to have their engagement announced. People would applaud. Some might even cheer. A couple of serving girls would toss confetti in the air. A new phase of her life would open. She ought to be excited. Instead, she had a sick feeling in the pit of her stomach.

"Get over it," she told herself roughly. She had to do what she had to do. There was no choice in the matter. But instead of a bride going to join her fiancé, she felt like a traitor going to her doom.

Was she doing the right thing? How could she know for sure?

She pressed both hands to her belly and thought of the child inside. The "right thing" was whatever was best for her baby. That, at least, was clear. Now if she could just be sure what that was, maybe she could stop feeling like a tightrope walker halfway across the rope.

And in the meantime, there was someone who seemed to take great delight in jiggling that rope she was so anxiously trying to get across.

CHAPTER FIVE

TURNING, PELLEA MARCHED into the library and confronted Monte.

He looked up and nodded as she approached. "She's a good one," he commented on Kimmee. "I'm glad you've got such a strong supporter nearby."

"Why didn't you tell me you'd seen her, actually chatted with her?" Pellea said, in no mood to be mollified. "Don't you see how dangerous that is? What if she talks?"

He eyed her quizzically. "You know her better than I do. What do you think? Will she?"

Pellea shook her head. "I don't know," she said softly. "I don't think so, but…"

She threw up her hands. It occurred to her how awful it was to live like this, always suspicious, always on edge. She wanted to trust her best friend. Actually, she did trust her. But knowing the penalty one paid for being wrong in this society kept her on her toes.

"Who knows?" she said, staring at him, wondering how this all would end.

It was tempting, in her darkest moments, to blame it

all on him. He came, he saw, he sent her into a frenzy of
excitement and—she had to face it—love, blinding her
to what was really going on, making her crazy, allowing
things to happen that should never have happened.

But he was just the temptor. She was the temptee.
From the very first, she should have stopped him in his
tracks, and she'd done nothing of the sort. In fact, she'd
immediately gone into a deep swoon and hadn't come
out of it until he was gone. She had no one to blame but
herself.

Still, she wished it was clearer just what he'd been
doing here two months ago, and why he'd picked her to
cast a spell over.

"Why did you come here to my chambers that first
time?" she asked him, getting serious. "That day you
found me by the fountain. What were you doing here?
What was your purpose? And why did you let me distract
you from it?"

He looked at her coolly. He'd finished the chicken
and eaten a good portion of the little loaf of bread. He
was feeling full and happy. But her questions were a bit
irksome.

"I came to get the lay of the land," he said, leaning
back in his chair. "And to see my ancestral castle. To
see my natural home." He looked a bit pained.

"The place I was created to rule," he added, giving it
emphasis that only confirmed her fears.

"See, I knew it," she said, feeling dismal. "You were
prepared to do something, weren't you?"

"Not then. Not yet." He met her gaze candidly. "But soon."

She shook her head, hands on her hips. "You want to send Leonardo and his entire family packing, don't you?" That was putting a pleasant face on something that might be very ugly, but she couldn't really face just how bad it could be.

He shrugged. "There's no denying it. It's been my obsession since I was a child." He gave her a riveting look. "Of course I'm going to take my country back. What else do I exist for?"

She felt faint. His obsession was her nightmare. She had to find a way to stop it.

"That is exactly where you go wrong," she told him, beginning to pace again. "Don't you see? You don't have to be royal. You don't have to restore your monarchy. Millions of people live perfectly happy lives without that."

He blinked at her as though he didn't quite get what she was talking about. "Yes, but do they make a difference? Do their lives have meaning in the larger scheme of things?"

She threw out her arms. "Of course they do. They fall in love and marry and have children and have careers and make friends and do things together and they're happy. They don't need to be king of anything." She appealed to him in all earnestness, wishing there was some way to convince him, knowing there was very little hope. "Why can't you be like that?"

He rose from the desk and she backed away quickly,

as though afraid he would try to take her in his arms again.

But he showed no intention of doing that. Instead, he began a slow survey of the books in her bookcases that lined the walls.

"You don't really understand me, Pellea," he said at last as he moved slowly through her collection. "I could live very happily without ever being king."

She sighed. "I wish I could believe that," she said softly.

He glanced back over his shoulder at her as she stood by the doorway, then turned to face her.

"I don't need to be king, Pellea. But there is something I do need." He went perfectly still and held her gaze with his own, his eyes burning.

"Revenge. I can never be fulfilled until I have my revenge."

She drew her breath in. Her heart beat hard, as though she was about to make a run for her life.

"That's just wicked," she said softly.

He held her gaze for a moment longer, then shrugged and turned away, shoving his hands down deep into his pockets and staring out into her miniature tropical forest.

"Then I'm wicked. I can't help it. Vengeance must be mine. I must make amends for what happened to my family."

She trembled. It was hopeless. His words felt like a dark and painful destiny to her. Like a forecast of doom.

There was no doubt in her mind that this would all end badly.

It was very true, what Monte had said. His character needed some kind of answer for what had happened to his family, some kind of retribution. Pellea knew that and on a certain level, she could hardly blame him. But didn't he see, and wasn't there any way she could make him see, that his satisfaction would only bring new misery for others? In order for him to feel relief, someone would have to pay very dearly.

"It's just selfish," she noted angrily.

He shrugged and looked at her coolly. "So I'm selfish. What else is new?"

She put her hand to her forehead and heaved a deep sigh. "There are those who live for themselves and their own gratification, and there are those who devote their lives to helping the downtrodden and the weak and oppressed. To make life better for the most miserable among us."

"You're absolutely right. You pay your money and you take your chances. I'd love to help the downtrodden and the poor and the oppressed in Ambria. Those are my people and I want to take care of them." He searched her eyes again. "But in order for me to do that, a few heads will have to roll."

The chimes on her elegant wall clock sounded and Pellea gasped.

"Oh, no! Look at the time. They're going to be here any minute. I wanted to get you out of here by now."

She looked around as though she didn't know where to hide him.

He stretched and yawned, comfortable as a cat, and then he rose and half sat on the corner of the desk. "It's all right. I'll just take a little nap while you're having your hair done."

"No, you will not!"

"As I remember it, your sleeping arrangements are quite comfortable. I think I'll spend a little quality time with your bedroom." He grinned, enjoying the outrage his words conjured up in her.

"I want you gone," she was saying fretfully, grabbing his arm for emphasis. "How do you get in here, anyway? Tell me how you do it. However you get in, that's the way you're going out. Tell me!"

He covered her hand with his own and caressed it. "I'll do better than that," he said, looking down at her with blunt affection. "I'll show you. But it will have to wait until we leave together."

She looked at his hand on hers. It felt hot and lovely. "I'm not going with you," she said in a voice that was almost a whimper.

"Yes, you are." He said it in a comforting tone.

Her eyes widened as she glanced up at him. He was doing it again—mesmerizing her. It was some sort of tantalizing magic and she had to resist it. "No, I'm not!" she insisted, but she couldn't gather the strength to pull her hand away.

He lifted her chin and kissed her softly on the lips.

"You are," he told her kindly. "You belong with me and you know it."

She felt helpless. Every time he touched her, she wanted to purr. She sighed in a sort of temporary surrender. "What are you going to do while I'm at the ball?" she asked.

"Don't worry. I'll find something to while away the time with." He raised an eyebrow. "Perfect opportunity, don't you think? To come and go at will."

She frowned. "There are guards everywhere. Surely you've seen that by now."

"Yes. But I do have your security setup to monitor things. That will help a lot."

"Oh." She groaned. She should never have let him see that.

She shook her head. "I should call the guards right now and take care of this once and for all."

"But you won't."

Suddenly, a surge of adrenaline gave her the spunk she needed to pull away from his touch, and once she was on her own, she felt emboldened again.

"Dare me!" she said, glaring at him with her hands on her hips.

He stared back at her for a long moment, then a slow grin spread over his handsome face. "I may be careless at times, my darling, but I'm not foolhardy. Even I know better than to challenge you like that."

The entry gong sounded. She sighed, all the fight ebbing out of her. "Just stay out of sight," she warned him. "I'll check in on you one last time before I go to the ball." She gave him a look of chagrin. "Unless, of course, you've left by then." She shrugged. "But I guess I won't hold my breath over that one."

He nodded. "Wise woman," he murmured as he watched her go. Then he slipped into her bedroom and closed the door before she'd let the hairdresser into the compound.

It was a beautiful room. The bedding was thick and luxurious, the headboard beautifully carved. Large oils of ancient landscapes, painted by masters of centuries past, covered the walls. He wondered what they had done with all the old portraits of his ancestors. Burned them, probably. Just another reason he needed his revenge.

But that was a matter to come. Right now he needed sleep.

He sat on the edge of her bed and looked at her bedside table, wondering what she was reading these days. What he saw gave him a bit of a jolt.

Beginning Pregnancy 101.

Interesting. It would seem Pellea was already thinking about having children. With Leonardo? That gave him a shudder. Surely she wasn't hoping to have a baby in order to reassure her father. That would be a step too far. And if she just had a yen for children, why choose Leonardo to have them with?

Making a face, he pushed the subject away. It was too depressing to give it any more attention.

He lay down on her sumptuous bed and groaned softly as he thought of the times he'd spent here. Two months ago everything had seemed so clean and simple.

A hungry man. A soft and willing woman. Great love-making. Good food. Luxurious surroundings. What could be better? He'd come back thinking it would all be easy to recreate. But he'd been dead wrong.

The wall clock struck the quarter hour again and tweaked a memory. There had been a huge, ancient grandfather clock in his mother's room when he was a child. There was a carved wooden tiger draped around the face of the timepiece and it had fascinated him. But even as he thought of that, he remembered that his mother had kept copies of her jewelry in a secret compartment in that clock.

What a strange and interesting castle this was. There were secret compartments and passageways and hiding places of all kinds just about everywhere. A few hundred years of the need to hide things had spurred his ancestors into developing ingenious and creative places to hide their most precious objects from the prying eyes and itching fingers of the servants and even of the courtiers. Life in the castle was a constant battle, it seemed, and it probably wasn't much different now.

Looking around Pellea's room, he wondered how many secret places had been found, and how many were still waiting, unused and unopened, after all these years. He knew of one, for sure, and that was the passageway that had brought him here twice now. He was pretty sure no one else had used it in twenty-five years. What else would he find if he tapped on a few walls and pressed on a few pieces of wood trim? It might be interesting to find out.

Later. Right now he needed a bit of sleep. Closing his eyes, he dreamed of Pellea and their nights together. He slept.

Pellea stood looking down at Monte, her heart so full of love, she had to choke back the tears that threatened. Tears would ruin her makeup and that was the last thing she would have been able to handle right now. She was on the edge of an emotional storm as it was.

Everyone had gone. She'd even sent the two men who were supposed to guard the tiara out into the hall to wait for her. And now she was ready to go and make the announcement that would set in stone her future life and that of her baby. But she needed just one more moment to look at the man she loved, the man she wished she were planning to marry.

If only they had met in another time, another place. If only circumstances were different. They could have been so happy together, the two of them. If there was no royalty for him to fight for, if her father was still as hale and hearty as he'd been most of her life, if her place weren't so precarious that she needed it bolstered by marrying Leonardo...

There were just too many things that would have to be different in order for things to work out the way they should, and for them to have a happy life. Unfortunately that didn't seem to be in the cards for her.

As for him—oh, he would get over it. He would never know that the baby she would have in a few months was really his. He was the only man she'd ever loved, but she had been very careful not to tell him that. She was pretty sure he'd had romances of one kind or another for years. It wouldn't be that hard for him. There would always be beautiful and talented women ready to throw themselves at him in a heartbeat.

Of course, if he did do as he threatened and try to take his country back by force, the entire question would be moot and they might all have to pay the ultimate price. Who knew?

In the meantime, she wanted just a moment more to watch him and dream….

When he woke an hour or so later, she was standing at the side of the bed. His first impression was benignness, but by the time he'd cleared his eyes, her expression had changed and she was glaring down at him.

"I don't know why you're still here," she said a bit mournfully. "Please don't get yourself killed while I'm at the ball."

He stretched and looked up at her sleepily. She was dressed to the hilt and the most beautiful thing he'd ever seen. His mother's tiara had been worked into a gorgeous coiffure that made her look as regal as any queen. Her creamy breasts swelled just above the neckline of her gown in old-fashioned allure. The bodice was tight, making her waist look tiny, as though he could reach out and pick her up with his two hands and pull her down…

His mouth went dry with desire and he reached for her. Deftly, she sidestepped his move and held him at bay.

"Don't touch," she warned. "I'm a staged work of art right now and I'm off to the photographer for pictures."

A piece of art was exactly what she was, looking just as she appeared before him. She could have walked right out of a huge portrait by John Singer Sargent, burnished lighting and rich velvet trimmings and all.

He sighed, truly pained. She looked good enough to ravish. But then she always did, didn't she?

"Forget the ball," he coaxed, though he knew it was all for naught. "Stay here with me. We'll lock the gate and recreate old times together."

"Right," she said, dismissing that out of hand, not even bothering to roll her eyes. She had other things on her mind right now. "The pictures will take at least an hour, I'm sure. Leonardo will meet me there and we'll go directly to the ball."

He frowned, feeling grumpy and overlooked for the moment. "Unless he has an unfortunate accident before he gets there," he suggested.

She looked at him sharply. "None of that, Monte. Promise me."

He stretched again and pouted. "When do you plan to make the big announcement?" he asked instead of making promises he might not be able to keep.

She frowned. "What does that matter?" she asked.

He grinned. "You are so suspicious of my every mood and plan."

Her eyes flashed. "With good reason, it seems."

He shrugged. "So I won't see you again until later?"

"No. Unless you decide to go away. As you should." She hesitated. She needed to make a few thing clear to him. He had to follow rules or she was going to have to get the guard to come help her keep him in line.

Right. That was a great idea. She made a face at herself. She was truly caught in a trap. She needed to keep him in line, but in order to do that, she would be signing his death warrant. There was no way that was going to happen.

At the same time, he showed no appreciation for the bind she was in. If he didn't feel it necessary to respect the rules she made, she couldn't have him here. He would have to understand that.

Taking a deep breath, she gave him the facts as she needed them to be.

"Once the announcement is made, our engagement will be official and there will be no more of anything like this," she warned him, a sweep of her hand indicating their entire relationship. "You understand that, don't you?"

His eyes were hooded as he looked up at her. "I understand what you're saying,"

"Monte, please don't do anything. You can't. I can't let you. Please have some respect."

His slow, insolent smile was his answer. "I would never do anything to hurt you."

She stared at him, then finally did roll her eyes. "Of

course not. Everything you do would be for my own good, wouldn't it?"

There was no escaping the tone of sarcasm in her voice. She sighed with exasperation and then the expression in her eyes changed. She hesitated. "Will you be gone?" she asked.

He met her gaze and held it. "Is that really what you hope?"

She started to say, "Of course," but then she stopped, bit her lip and sighed. "How can I analyze what I'm hoping right now?" she said instead, her voice trembling. "How can I even think clearly when you're looking at me like that?"

One last glare and she whirled, leaving the room as elegantly as any queen might do.

He rose and followed, going to the doorway so that he could watch her leave her chambers, a uniformed guard on either side. She could have been royalty from another century. She could have been Anne Boleyn on her way to the tower. He thought she was pretty special. He wanted her to be his, but just how that would work was not really clear.

Right now he had a purpose in mind—exploring the other side of the castle where his family's living quarters had been. That was the section that had burned and he knew it had been recently renovated. He only hoped enough would be left of what had been so that he could find something he remembered.

It would seem the perfect time to do it. With the ball beginning, no one would be manning their usual places.

Everyone would be gravitating toward the ballroom for a look at the festivities. A quick trip to Pellea's surveillance room was in order, and then he would take his chances in the halls.

The long, tedious picture-taking session was wrapping up and Pellea waited with Kimmee for Leonardo to come out. The photographers were taking a few last individual portraits of him.

"Shall I go check on the preparations for your entrance to the ballroom?" Kimmee asked, and Pellea nodded her assent.

It had been her experience that double-checking never hurt and taking things for granted usually led to disaster. Besides, she needed a moment to be alone and settle her feelings.

Turning slowly, she appraised herself in the long, full-length mirror. Was that the face of a happy woman? Was that the demeanor of a bride?

Not quite. But it was the face of a rather regal-looking woman, if she did say so herself. But why was she even thinking such a thing? She would never be queen, no matter what. Monte might be king someday, but he would never pick her to be his wife. He couldn't pick someone from a traitor's family to help him rule Ambria, now could he?

The closest she would get to that was to marry Leonardo. Did that really matter to her? She searched her soul, looking for even the tiniest hint of ambition and couldn't find it. That sort of thing was important to her father, but not to her. If her father weren't involved, she would leave with Monte and never look back. But that was impossible under the circumstances.

Still, it was nice to dream about. What if she and Monte were free? They might get on a yacht and sail to the South Seas and live on an island. Not an island like Ambria with its factions always in contention and undermining each other. A pretty island with coconut trees and waterfalls, a place that was quiet and warm and peaceful with turquoise waters and silver-blue fish and white-sand beaches.

But there was no time to live in dreams. She had to live in the here and now. And that meant she had to deal with Leonardo.

She smiled at him as he came out of the sitting room.

"All done?" she asked.

"So it seems," he replied, then leaned close. "Ah, so beautiful," he murmured as he tried to nuzzle her neck.

"Don't touch," she warned him, pulling back.

"Yes, yes, I know. You're all painted up and ready to go." He took her hand and kissed her fingers. "But I want to warn you, my beauty, I plan to touch you a lot on our wedding night."

That sent a chill down her spine. She looked at him in surprise. He'd never shown any sexual interest in her before. This put an ominous pall on her future, didn't it? She'd heard lurid tales about his many mistresses and she'd assumed that he knew their marriage would be for advantage and convenience only, and not for love or for anything physical. Now he seemed to be having second thoughts. What was going on here?

She glanced at Kimmee who'd just returned and had heard him as well, and they exchanged a startled glance.

Leonardo took a call on his mobile, then snapped it shut and frowned. "I'm sorry, my love," he told her. "I'm afraid I'm going to have to let the guards escort you to the ballroom. I'll be along later. I have a matter that must be taken care of immediately."

Something in his words sent warning signals through her.

"What is it, Leonardo?" she asked, carefully putting on a careless attitude. "Do we need to man the barricades?"

"Nothing that should trouble you, my sweet," he said, giving her a shallow smile that didn't reach his eyes. "It seems we may have an interloper in the castle."

"Oh?" Her blood ran cold and she clenched her fists behind the folds of her skirt. "What sort of interloper?"

He waved a hand in the air. "It may be nothing, but a few of the guards seem to think they saw a stranger on one of the monitors this afternoon." He shook his head. "We don't allow intruders in the castle, especially on a night like this."

He sighed. "I just have to go and check out what they caught on the recorder. I'll be back in no time."

"Hurry back, my dear," she said absentmindedly,

thinking hard about how she was going to warn
Monte.

"I will, my love." He bowed in her direction and
smiled at her. "Don't do any dancing without me," he
warned. Turning, he disappeared out the door.

Pellea reached out to steady herself to keep from keel-
ing over. She met Kimmee's gaze and they both stared
at each other with worried eyes.

"I told him to go," she fretted to her lifelong friend
and servant. "Now he's probably out running around the
castle and about to get caught. Oh, Kimmee!"

Kimmee leaned close. "Don't worry, Pel," she whispered, scanning the area to make sure no one could
overhear them. "I'll find him and I'll warn him. You
can count on me."

Pellea grabbed her arm. "Tell him there is no more
room for error. He has to get out of the castle right
now!"

"I will. Don't you worry. He'll get the message."

And she dashed off into the hallway.

Pellea took a deep breath and tried to quiet her nerves.
She had to forget all about Monte and the trouble he
might be in. She had to act as though everything were
normal. In other words, she would have to pretend. And
it occurred to her that this might be a lesson for the way
things would be for the rest of her life.

CHAPTER SIX

MONTE WAS BACK FROM EXPLORING and he was waiting impatiently for Kimmee to make good on her promises and show up with a costume he could wear to the ball.

He'd been to the other side of the castle and he'd seen things that would take him time to assimilate and deal with emotionally. It could have been overwhelming if he'd let it be. He'd barely skimmed through the area and not much remained of the home he'd lived in with his loving family. Most of what was rebuilt had a new, more modern cast.

But he had found something important. He'd found a storeroom where some of the rescued items and furniture from his family's reign had been shoved aside and forgotten for years. A treasure trove that he would have to explore when he got the chance. But in the short run, he'd found his mother's prized grandfather clock. More important, he'd found her secret compartment, untouched after all these years. That alone had given him a sense of satisfaction.

And one of the items he had found in that secret

hiding place was likely to come in very handy this very night.

But right now, he just wanted to see Kimmee appear in the gateway. He knew she'd been helping with the photo shoot, but surely that was over by now. If she didn't come soon, he would have to find a way to go without a special costume—and that would be dangerous enough to make him think at least twice.

"Don't give up on me!"

Kimmee's voice rang out before the gong sounded and she came rushing in bearing bulky gifts and a wide smile.

"I've got everything you need right here," she claimed, spreading out her bounty before him. "Though I'm afraid it's all for naught."

"Once more, you save the day," he told her as he looked through the items, thoroughly impressed. "I'm going to have to recommend you for a medal."

"A reward for costume procurement?" she asked with a laugh. "But there's more. I'm afraid you won't be able to use this after all."

"No?" He stopped and looked at her. "Why not?"

"The castle is on stranger alert." She sighed. "You must have gone exploring because some of the guards claim they saw you—or somebody—on one of the hall monitors."

"Oh. Bad luck."

She shrugged. "Leonardo is looking into it and he seems pretty serious about it. So Pellea sent me to tell you to get out while the getting's good, because there's no time left." She shook her head, looking at him earnestly. "I went ahead and brought you the costume, because I promised I would, and I knew you'd want to see this. But I don't think it would be wise to use it. You're going to have to go, and go quickly."

"Am I?" He held up the coat to the uniform and gazed at it.

"Oh, I think you'd better," she said.

"And I will." He smiled at her. "All in good time. But first, I want to dance with Pellea."

Her face was filled with doubt but her eyes were shining. "But if you get caught...?"

"Then I'll just have to get away again," he told her. "But I don't plan to get caught. I've got a mask, don't I? No one will be sure who I really am, and I'll keep a sharp eye out." He grinned. "Don't worry about me. I'm going to go try this on."

"Well, what do you know?" She sighed, wary but rather happy he wasn't going to give up so easily. "Go ahead and try it on. I'll wait and help with any last-minute adjustments."

He took the costume up as though it were precious—and in a way it was. He recognized what she'd found for him—the official dress uniform of Ambrian royalty from the nineteenth century—a uniform one of his great-great-grandfathers had probably worn. He slipped into it quickly. It all fitted like a glove. Looking in the mirror, he had to smile. He looked damn good in gold braid and a stiff collar. As though he was born to wear it.

When he walked out, Kimmee applauded, delighted with how it had worked out.

"Here's your mask," she said, handing it to him. "As you say, it will be very important in keeping your identity hidden. And it's a special one. Very tight. Very secure." She gave it a sharp test, pulling on the band at the back. "No one will be able to pull it off."

"Exactly what I need. Kimmee, you're a genius."

"I am, aren't I?" She grinned, pleased as punch. "Believe me, sir, I take pride in my work—underhanded as it may be."

He shook his head. "I don't consider this underhanded at all."

And actually, she agreed. "I'll just think of it this way—anything I can do to help you is for the good of the country."

He looked at her closely, wondering if she realized who he was. But her smile was open and bland. If she knew, she wasn't going to let it out. Still, it was interesting that she'd put it that way.

"I've got to hurry back," she said as she started toward the gate. "I'm helping in the ladies' powder room. You pick up all the best rumors in there."

"Ah, the ladies like to talk, do they?" he responded, adjusting his stand-up collar.

"They like to impress each other and they forget that we servants can hear, too." She gave him a happy wave. "I'll let you know if anything good turns up."

He nodded. "The juicier the better."

She laughed as she left, and he sobered. He'd been

lighthearted with Kimmee, but in truth, this was quite an emotional experience for him.

He took one last look in the mirror. For the first time in many years, he felt as if he'd found something he really belonged to, something that appealed to his heart as well as his head. It was almost a feeling of coming home.

And home was what he'd missed all these years. Without real parents, without a real family, he'd ached for something of his own.

He'd had an odd and rather disjointed life. For his first eight years, he'd been the much beloved, much cosseted Crown Prince of Ambria, living in the rarified air of royal pomp and celebrity. His mother and father had doted on him. He'd shown every evidence of being as talented and intelligent as his position in life warranted, and also as pleasant and handsome as a prince should be. Everyone in his milieu was in awe of him. The newspapers and magazines were full of pictures of him—his first steps, his first puppy, his new Easter clothes, his first bicycle. It was a charmed life.

And then came the coup. He still remembered the night the castle burned, could still smell the fire, feel the fear. He'd known right away that his parents were probably dead. For an eight-year-old boy, that was a heavy burden to bear.

That night, as he and his brother Darius were rushed away from the castle and hustled to the continent in a rickety boat, he'd looked back and seen the fire, and even at his young age, he'd known his way of life was crumbling into dust just as surely as the castle of his royal ancestors was.

He and Darius were quickly separated and wouldn't see each other again until they were well into adulthood. For the first few weeks after his escape, he was passed from place to place by agents of the Ambrian royalty, always seeing new contacts, never sure who these people were or why he was with them. People were afraid to be associated with him, yet determined to keep him safe.

As the regime's crown prince, he was in special danger. The Granvillis had taken over Ambria and it was known that they had sent agents out to find all the royal children and kill them. They didn't want any remnants of the royal family around to challenge their rule.

Monte finally found himself living in Paris with an older couple, the Stephols, who had ties to the monarchy but also a certain distance that protected them from scrutiny. At first, he had to hide day and night, but after a year or so, the Stephols got employment with the foreign service and from then on, they were constantly moving from one assignment to another, and Monte lived all over the world, openly claiming to be their child.

He grew up with the best of everything—elite private schools, vacations in Switzerland, university training in business. But he was always aware that he was in danger and had to keep his real identity a secret. The couple treated him with polite reserve and not a lot of affection—as though he were a museum piece they were protecting from vandals but would return to its proper shelf when the time came. They had no other children and were sometimes too cool for comfort. The couple was very closely knit and Monte often felt like an interloper—which he probably was. They were kind to him, but somewhat reserved, and it was a lonely life. They obviously knew he was special, though he wasn't sure if they knew exactly who he was.

He knew, though. He remembered a lot and never forgot his family, his country or that he was royal. That in itself made him careful. He remembered the danger, still had nightmares about it. As he got older, it was hard not being able to talk to anyone about his background, not having someone he could question, but he read everything he could about his homeland and began to understand why he had to maintain his anonymity. He knew that some saw him as cold and removed from normal emotions. That wasn't true. His emotions were simmering inside, ready to explode when the time was right.

Coming back to Ambria had done a lot to help put things in order in his mind. Finding Pellea had confused the issue a bit, but he thought he could handle that. Now, putting on the uniform that should have been his by rights cemented a feeling of belonging in him. He was the Crown Prince of Ambria, and he wanted his country back.

Monte DeAngelis, Crown Prince of Ambria, walked into the ballroom annex in a uniform that reflected his position, and he did it proudly. He knew the authorities were looking for him and it would only take one careless action, one moment of inattention, to make them realize he was the intruder they were searching for.

But he was willing to risk it. He had to. He needed to do this and he was counting on his natural abilities and intelligence to keep him from harm. After all, he'd had to count on exactly those for most of his life, and his talents had so far stood him in good stead. Now for the ultimate test. He definitely expected to pass it.

The announcer looked up at him in surprise and frowned, knowing that he'd never seen this man before in his life. He got up from his chair and came over busily, carrying papers and trying to look as though he were comfortably in charge.

"Welcome," he said shortly, with a bow. "May I have the name to be announced?"

Monte stood tall and smiled at him.

"Yes, you may. Please announce me as the Count of Revanche," he said with an appropriately incomprehensible Mediterranean accent, though he was blatantly using the French word for revenge.

The man blinked, appearing puzzled. "And Revanche is…?"

"My good man, you've never visited our wonderful region?" Monte looked shocked. "We're called the wine country of the southern coast. You must make a visit on your next holiday."

"Oh," the man responded dutifully, still baffled. "Of course." He bowed deeply and held out his arm with a flourish. "If you please, Your Highness."

He reached for the loudspeaker and made the announcement.

"Ladies and gentleman, may I present His Highness, the Count of Revanche?"

And Monte held his head high as he navigated the steep stairway into the ballroom.

Heads turned. And why not? Obviously, no one had ever heard of him before, and yet he was a commanding presence. He could see the wave of whispering his entrance had set off, but he ignored it, looking for Pellea.

He picked her out of the crowd quickly enough. For a moment the sight of all those masks blinded him, but he found her and once he'd done that, she was all he could see. She stood in the midst of a small group of women and it seemed to him as though a spotlight shone down on her. In contrast to the others around her, the mask she wore was simple, a smooth black accent that set off the exotic shape of her dark eyes and allowed the sparkling jewels of the tiara to take center stage. At the same time, the porcelain translucence of her skin, the delicate set of her jaw, the lushness if her lips, all added to the stunning picture she made in her gorgeous gown. She was so utterly beautiful, his heart stopped in his chest.

He began to head in her direction, but he didn't want to seem over-anxious, so he made a few bows and gave out a few smiles along the way.

Only a few stately couples were dancing as he entered the cavernous room, but he knew how this sort of ball operated, having been to enough of them on the continent. The older people did most of the dancing at first, and the music was calm and traditional. Then the younger ones would filter in. By a certain hour, rocking rhythms and Latin beats would be the order of the day, and the older people would have retreated to drink in the bar or queue for the midnight buffet table.

That was the structure, but it wasn't really relevant to his plans. He just wanted Pellea in his arms. Now all he had to do was to get there and claim her.

Many of the women had noticed him right away. In fact, a few were blatantly looking him over. One pretty little redhead had actually lowered her mask in order to wink at him in outright invitation.

Meanwhile, Pellea hadn't even noticed his arrival. She was deep in conversation with another woman, both of them very earnest. It was quite evident that the subject of their talk was more likely to be the state of world affairs than the latest tart recipe. But what did that matter? She was looking so beautiful, if one had to pick out a queen from the assemblage, she would take the night.

Why did that thought keep echoing in his mind? He turned away, reminding himself that the question was out of order. He wasn't going to think about anything beyond the dancing tonight. And in order to get things started, he decided to take the little redhead up on her offer.

She accepted his invitation like a shot and very soon they were on the dance floor. It was a Viennese waltz, but they managed to liven it up considerably. She chatted away but he hardly heard a word she said. His attention was all on Pellea.

As he watched, Leonardo asked her to dance, and she refused him, shaking her head. He looked a bit disgruntled as he walked away, but his friends crowded around him and in a moment, they all went straight for the hard liquor bar, where he quickly downed a stiff one.

Monte smiled. Fate seemed to be playing right into his hands. The music ended and Monte returned the redhead to her companions. He gave her a smile, but not many words to cherish after he was gone. Turning, he headed straight toward Pellea.

As he approached, she looked up and he saw her eyes widen with recognition behind her mask. She knew who he was right away, and that disappointed him. He'd hoped to get a bit of play out of the costume and mask before he had to defend himself for showing up here.

But then he realized the truth, and it warmed his heart. They would know each other in the dark, wouldn't they?

Not to say that she was pleased to see him.

"You!" she hissed at him, eyes blazing. "Are you crazy? What are you doing here?"

"Asking the most stunning woman in the room to dance with me." He gave her a deep bow. "May I have the honor?"

"No!" She glared at him and lifted her fan to her face. She was obviously finding it hard to show her anger to him and hide it from the rest of the people in the room at the same time. "Didn't Kimmee tell you that you'd been seen?" she whispered.

"Kimmee delivered your message and I acknowledge it. But I won't be cowed by it." He gave her a flourish and a flamboyant smile that his mask couldn't hide. "I have a life to live you know."

"And this stupid ball is that important to your life?" she demanded, trying to keep her voice down and astounded that he could be so careless.

Didn't he care? Or did he see himself as some kind of superhero, so over-confident in his own abilities that he scoffed at danger? In any case, it was brainless and dangerous and it made her crazy.

"Oh, yes, this ball is very important," he answered her question. His smile was slow and sensual. "It may be my last chance to dance with you. Believe me, Pellea, there is nothing more important than that."

She was speechless, then angry. How did he do it, again and again? Somehow he always touched her emotions, even when she knew very well that was exactly what he was aiming at. She felt like a fool, but she had to admit, a part of her that she wasn't very proud of loved it.

Monte knew he'd weakened her defenses with that one and he smiled. It might sound glib and superficial, but he meant every word of it.

She was beautiful, from head to toe, and as he gazed at the way the tiara worked perfectly with her elaborate ensemble, he thought about his memories of his own mother wearing it, and a mist seemed to cloud his eyes for a moment. In many ways, Pellea fitted into the continuity of culture here in Ambria the way no other woman he'd ever met could do. It was something to keep in mind, wasn't it?

Out of the corner of his eye, he saw Leonardo coming back into the room and looking their way, frowning fiercely. Monte smiled and glanced at Pellea. She'd seen him, too.

"We'd better get out on the dance floor or we'll be answering questions from Leonardo in no time," he noted. "He has that mad inquisitioner look to him tonight."

Quickly, she nodded and raised her arms. He took her into his embrace and they began to sway to the music.

"This is all so wrong," she murmured, leaning against his shoulder. "You know this is only going to anger him."

He glanced over at Leonardo, who was scowling, his friends gathered around him. Angering Leonardo was the least of his worries right now. He was gambling that the man wouldn't see him as the intruder he'd been studying on the castle monitoring system.

If he'd arrived in more normal attire, that might have been a problem. But because he'd appeared in such an elaborate costume, claimed to be royal and seemed to fit so well with the others who were here, he hoped Leonardo wouldn't connect him with the intruder until it was too late.

At first glance, he would have to say that he'd been right. Everything was influenced by context.

"I see that your handsome and valorous swain is celebrating his fool head off tonight," he noted as Leonardo threw back another shot of Scotch.

"Yes," she whispered. "He's already had too much. It's becoming a habit of his lately. I'm going to have to work on that."

He gazed down at her and barely contained the sneer he felt like using at her words. "Are you?"

"Yes." She lifted her chin and met his gaze defiantly. "After we're married."

She said the word loud and clear, emphasizing it to make sure he got her drift. And now he did sneer. He got it all right. He just didn't want to accept it.

He whirled her in a fancy turn, then dipped her in a way that took her breath away. But she was half laughing at the same time.

"Oh, that was lovely," she told him, clinging to him in a way that sent his pulse soaring.

"Your lover boy didn't like it," he told her blithely.

"Maybe not," she admitted, looking back at where Leonardo was standing a bit apart from his friends and watching her. "But you have to admit, until you arrived, all in all, he seems to be happy tonight."

"Why wouldn't he be?" He pulled her up against his chest and held her there for a beat too long, enjoying the soft, rounded feel of her body against his. "And you, my darling," he added softly. "Are you happy?"

Her dark eyed gaze flickered up at him, then away again. "You know the answer to that. But I'm prepared to do my duty."

That was an answer that infuriated him and he was silent for a moment, trying to control himself. But he couldn't stay angry with her in his arms. He looked down at her and his heart swelled. When was he going to admit it? This trip had been completely unnecessary. He'd already gathered all the reconnaissance data he needed on his last visit to Ambria. He'd only come for one thing. Trying to turn it into a Helen-of-Troy kidnapping of the enemy's most beautiful woman was just fanciful rationalizing. He'd come to find Pellea because he needed to see her. That was all there was to it. But now that he knew about this insane wedding to a Granvilli monster, he wanted to get her out of here with more urgency. She had to go. She couldn't marry Leonardo. What a crime against nature that would be!

And yet, there was the problem of her father. No matter what he might think of the man, if he ripped her away from him by force, without first convincing her to go, she would never forgive him. Knowing how important family was, and how traumatic it could be when it was torn apart, he might never forgive himself.

He had to find a way to make her come with him. Somehow.

He dipped her again, pulling her in close and bending over her in a rather provocative way. "I promise you, Pellea," he said, his voice rough and husky. "I swear it on my parents' graves. You will be happy."

Her heart was beating hard. She stared at him, not sure what he was up to. He was making promises he couldn't possibly keep. She didn't believe a word of it.

"You can't decide on my happiness," she told him bluntly. "It's not up to you."

"Of course not," he said, his bitterness showing. "I suppose it's up to your father, isn't it?"

She drew her breath in and let resentment flow through her for a moment. Then she pushed it back. It did no good to let emotions take over at a time like this.

"I know you hate my father," she said softly, "and you may have good reason to, from your point of view."

"You mean from a reasonable perspective?"

She ignored his taunt and went on.

"But I don't hate him. I love him very much. My mother died when I was very young and he and I have been our only family ever since. He's been everything to me. I love him dearly."

He pulled back, still holding her loosely in his arms. "You'd choose him over me?" he asked, his voice rough as sandpaper.

Her eyes widened. His words startled her. In fact, he took her breath away with the very concept. What was he asking of her? Whatever he was thinking, he had no right to put it to her that way.

And so she nodded. "Of course I would choose him. He and I have a real relationship. With you, I have..."

Her voice trailed off. Even now she was reluctant to analyze what exactly it was that they had together. "With you I had something that was never meant to last," she said finally.

He stared at her, wondering why her words stung so deeply. Wondering why there was an urge down in him that was clawing its way to the surface, an urge to do what he'd only bantered about, an urge to throw her over his shoulder as his own personal trophy, and fight his way out of the castle.

Kidnap her. That was the answer. He would carry her off and hide her away somewhere only he could find her. The need swelled inside him, almost choking him with its intensity. He was flying high on fantasy.

But he came back down to earth with a thump. What the hell was wrong with him? That whole scenario was just sick. He had no more right to force her into anything than he had to force anyone. If he really wanted her that badly, he would have to find a way to convince her to want him just as much. And so far, that wasn't working.

She preferred to stay with her father.

But that wasn't fair, to put it that way. Her father was her only living relative and he was very ill. Of course she was protective of him and wanted to stay with him. Her tenderness and compassion were part of what he loved about her.

"So I guess I come in third," he mentioned with deceptive calm. "Behind your father and Leonardo." He glanced back at her fiancé waiting for this long dance to end. "Maybe I ought to have a talk with your lover boy."

She drew her breath in sharply. "Stay away from him, Monte. The more he drinks the more dangerous he'll be."

She was passionate and worried, but also confused and torn and not at all sure how to handle this. Here she was in the same room with the man she loved and even in his arms, and just a stone's throw away from the man she was pledged to marry.

Let's face it, he was the man she *had* to marry, no way around it. She was pregnant. She needed a husband. Without one, she would be persona non grata in this community. And if those in charge ever figured out who the baby's father was, her child would be an outcast as well.

She really didn't have much choice in the matter. In a country like this, living in this rarefied sliver of the society as she did, and caring for her father as she did, there was no option to play the free spirit and defy the culture's norms. She needed protection. It was all very well to love Monte, but he would never marry her. She had to provide for her child—and herself. No one else was prepared to do it for her.

No one but Leonardo, and for that—though Monte might never understand it—she would be forever grateful to the man.

Leonardo knew she was pregnant, though he didn't know who the father was. He didn't really care. It wasn't love he was looking for in their relationship. It was the factions she represented, the power she could help him assemble, and the prestige of her name. Though her father had been mistrusted for a time because he had worked with the old DeAngelis regime, years had passed now, and his reputation was clear. Now, the magic of the old days and the old regime was what mattered. People were said to hold him in such high esteem, his reputation rivaled that of the Granvillis. And that was one reason Leonardo wanted her on his side.

It was well understood between the two of them. She was getting something she needed from him and he was getting something he needed from her. If Monte had just stayed away, everything would be going along as planned.

But Monte had appeared out of nowhere once again and upset the apple cart. She loved him. She couldn't deny it. And he was the father of her child, although he didn't know it. And here he was, inserting himself into the equation in a way that was sure to bring misery to them all. Did she have the strength to stop him? So far, it didn't seem possible.

The music finally came to an end. She knew Leonardo was waiting for her to return to her spot and she was resigned to it. Reluctantly, she began to slip out of Monte's arms.

But he didn't want to let her go.

"Do you find it oppressively hot in here?" he murmured close to her ear, his warm breath tickling her skin.

"Oh, I don't know, I guess…"

He didn't wait for a full answer. In the confusion of couples coming and going every which way to get on and off the dance floor, he maneuvered her right out the open French doors onto the dimly lit and almost empty terrace. As the small orchestra struck up a new tune, they continued their dance.

"Monte," she remonstrated with him. "You can't do

this. You're not the only one who wants to dance with me, you know."

"I know that very well," he said. "Why do you think I felt I had to resort to these guerilla tactics to have my way with you?"

She laughed low in her throat and he pulled her into the shadows and kissed her. His kiss was music by Mozart, sculpture by Michelangelo, the dancing of Fred Astaire. He was the best.

Of course, she wasn't exactly an expert on such things. Her experience wasn't extensive. But she'd had make-out sessions with incredibly attractive men in her time, and she knew this was top-tier kissing.

He started slowly, just barely nipping at her lips, and, as she felt herself enjoying the sensation and reaching for more of it, he found his way into the honey-sweet heat of her mouth, using his tongue to explore the terrain and sample the most tender and sensitive places.

She knew she was being hypnotized again and for the moment, she didn't care. His slow, provocative touch was narcotic, and she fell for the magic gladly. If he had picked her up and carried her off at that moment, she wouldn't have protested at all.

But he'd kept the clearer head and he pulled back.

"Oh, Monte, no," she sighed, the sweetness of his lips still branding hers. She felt so wonderful in his arms, like a rose petal floating downstream. The music, the cool night air, his strong arms around her—what could be better?

"Please," she whispered, reaching for him again.

"Not now, my darling," he whispered back, nuzzling behind her ear. "There are people nearby. And there are things that must be done."

"Like what?" she murmured rather sulkily, but she was beginning to come back to her senses as well and she sighed, realizing that he was perfectly right to deflect her. "Oh, bother," she muttered, annoyed with herself as her head cleared. "There you go, flying me to the moon again."

He laughed softly, dropping one last kiss on her lips. "There will be plenty of time for that later," he promised.

"No there won't," she said sensibly. "I'll be married. And if you think you're going to be hanging around once that has happened, you'd better think again."

She couldn't help but wince as she let herself imagine just how bereft her world was going to be.

But she managed to keep a fiercely independent demeanor. "There are certain lines I swear I will never cross."

He gazed at her, his blue eyes clouded and unreadable. "What time is the announcement planned for?" he asked her.

She looked up at him in surprise. "Just before the midnight buffet," she answered, then frowned, alarmed. "Wait. Monte! What are you planning to do?"

"Who, me? Why would you think I was planning anything at all?"

"Because I know you." She planted her hands on his

shoulders and shook him. "Don't do it! Whatever you're planning, don't!"

He pretended to be wounded by her suspicion, though his eyes were sparkling with laughter. "I can't believe you have so little faith in me," he said.

She started to respond, but then her gaze caught sight of something that sent her pulse racing. "Leonardo," she whispered to Monte. "He's found us."

"Oh, good," he said. "I've been wanting to talk to him."

CHAPTER SEVEN

PELLEA DREW IN A SHARP BREATH, filled with dread as she watched Leonardo approach.

"I'll hold him off if you want to make a run for it," she told Monte urgently, one hand gripping his shoulder. "But go quickly!"

"Why would I run?" he said, turning to meet the man, still holding her other hand. "I've been looking forward to this."

"Oh, Monte," she whimpered softly, wishing she could cast a spell and take them anywhere else.

Leonardo's face was filled with a cold fury that his silver mask couldn't hide.

"Unhand my fiancée, sir," he ordered, his lip curling and one hand on the hilt of the sword at his side. "And identify yourself, if you please."

Monte's smile was all pure, easy confidence. "You don't allow hand holding with old friends?" he asked, holding Pellea's hand up where Leonardo could see his fingers wrapped around hers. "Pellea and I have a special connection, but it's nothing that should concern you."

"A special connection?" Leonardo repeated, seeming momentarily uncertain. "In what way?"

"Family connections," Monte explained vaguely. "We go way back." But he dropped her hand and clicked his heels before giving Leonardo a stiff little bow. "Allow me to introduce myself. I'm the Count of Revanche. Perhaps you've heard of me?"

Leonardo looked a bit puzzled, but much of his fury had evaporated and a new look of interest appeared on his long face. "Revanche, is it?"

"Yes." Monte stuck out his hand and gave the man a broad smile. It was fascinating how the hint of royalty always worked magic, especially with dictator types. They always seemed a little starstruck by a title, at least at first. He only hoped the sense of awe would last long enough to save him from ending up in a jail cell.

"It is a pleasure to meet you at last, Leonardo," he said heartily. "I've heard so much about you. I'm hoping the reality can compete with the legend."

Leonardo hesitated only a moment, then stuck out his own hand and Monte shook it warmly.

"Have I heard of you before?" he asked.

Monte gave a grand shrug. "That's as may be. But I've heard of you." He laughed as though that was quite a joke. "Your father and I go way back."

"My father?" Leonardo brightened. "How so?"

Monte nodded wisely. "He's meant a great deal to me in my life. In fact, I wouldn't be the man I am today without his strong hand in my early training."

"Ah, I see." Leonardo began to look downright welcoming. "So he has mentored you in some way."

Monte smiled. "One might say that. We were once thick as thieves."

Leonardo actually smiled. "Then you will be happy to know he is going to make an appearance here tonight."

Monte's confidence slipped just a bit, but he didn't let it show. "Is he? What a treat it will be to see him again. I'll be happy to have a drink with him."

"Well, why not have a drink with me while we await his arrival?" Leonardo suggested. He was obviously warming to this visiting count and had forgotten all about the manhandling of his future bride. "Come along, Pellea," he said, sweeping them back into the ballroom with him. "We must make sure our guest is well supplied with refreshment."

Her gaze met Monte's and she bit her lip. She could see what he was doing, but she didn't like it at all. The moment an opportunity arose, she would help him make a run for it. That was the only thing she could see that would save him. This manly bonding thing couldn't last once the truth began to seep out.

But Monte gave her a wink and his eyes crackled with amusement. He was obviously having the time of his life fooling someone who didn't even realize he was dealing with his worst enemy.

They made their way to the bar, and by the time they got there, a crowd of Leonardo's friends and hangers-on had joined them.

"Come," Leonardo said expansively. "We must drink together."

"Of course," Monte agreed cordially. "What are we drinking?"

The bartender slapped a bottle of something dark and powerful-looking on the bar and everyone cheered.

"We must share a toast," Monte said, holding his glass high. "Let us drink to destiny."

"To destiny!"

Each man downed his drink and looked up happily for more. The bartender obliged.

"And to fathers everywhere," Monte said, holding his glass up again. "And to General Georges Granvilli in particular."

"Well. Why not?" Leonardo had just about decided Monte was the best friend he'd ever had by now. He pounded him on the back at every opportunity and merrily downed every drink Monte put before him.

Pellea watched this spectacle in amazement. But when Monte offered her a glass, she shook her head.

"Pellea, come share a toast with us," he coaxed, trying to tempt her. "I'll get you something fruity if you like."

She shook her head firmly. "No. I don't drink."

He blinked at her, remembering otherwise and sidling a bit closer. "You drank happily enough two months ago," he said to her quietly. "We practically bathed in champagne, as I remember. What's changed?"

She flashed him a warning look. "That was then. This is now."

He frowned, ready to take that up and pursue an answer, but Leonardo wrapped an arm around his neck and proclaimed, "I love you, man."

"Of course," Monte said with a sly smile. "You and I are like blood brothers."

Pellea blanched. Was she the only one who got a chill at hearing his words?

"Blood brothers." Leonardo had imbibed too much to be able to make head nor tails of that, but it sounded good to him.

Monte watched him with pity. "You don't understand that," he allowed. "I'm going to have to explain it to you. But for now, trust me." He raised his glass into the light, glad no one seemed to notice that he had never actually drunk what was in it. "Blood brothers under the skin."

"Are we, by God?" Leonardo was almost in tears at the thought.

"Yes," Monte said with an appropriate sense of irony. "We are."

Pellea shook her head. She could see where this was inevitably going and knew there would probably be no announcement of their engagement tonight. Unless Monte volunteered to prop the man up for it, and that wasn't likely.

All in all, this appeared to be a part of his plan. Didn't he understand that it would do no good? The announcement would be made, one way or another, before the wedding, and that was only two days away. He couldn't stop it. She couldn't let him.

He caught her eye, gesturing for her to come closer.

"Do you think Georges will really make an appearance?" he whispered to her.

She shook her head. "I have no idea. I haven't seen him in months. They always say he is in France, taking the waters for his health. For all I know, he's been right here this whole time, watching television in his room."

Monte glanced at Leonardo, who was laughing uproariously with a couple of his mates. One more toast and it was pretty obvious he wouldn't be capable of making an engagement announcement.

"Wait here, my love," he said softly. "I have to finish what I've started."

"Monte, no!" She grabbed his arm to keep him with her, but he pulled away and joined the men at the bar.

"A final toast," he offered to Leonardo. "To our new and everlasting friendship."

"Our friendship!" cried Leonardo, turning up his glass and taking in the contents in one gulp. Then, slowly, he put the glass down. Staring straight ahead, his eyes glassy, he began to crumble. His knees went first, and then his legs. Monte and a couple of the others grabbed him before he hit the ground. A sigh went through the crowd. And, at the same time, bugles sounded in the hallway.

"The General is coming!" someone cried out. "It's General Georges."

"Prepare for the arrival of the General."

Shock went through the crowd in waves, as though no one knew exactly what to do, but all realized something had to be done. Their leader was coming. He had to be welcomed in style.

One of Leonardo's friends sidled up to Monte. "We've got to get him out of here before his father comes," he whispered urgently. "There'll be hell to pay. Believe me, the old man will kill him."

Monte looked at the limp young gentleman who thought he was going to marry Pellea and had a moment of indecision. What did he care if Georges saw his son like this? It wasn't his problem.

And yet, in a way, it *was* his fault. Leonardo was not his enemy. His rival, yes. But it was Leonardo's father who was his mortal enemy. And perhaps it would be just as well if Georges wasn't distracted by focusing his rage on his hapless son.

Because he did plan to face him. How could he avoid the confrontation he'd spent his life preparing for?

"Let's go," he said to the man who'd approached him. "Let's get him to his chambers before his father gets here."

He looked back at Pellea, signaling her to his intentions. But she wasn't paying attention any longer. A servant had come to find her.

"My lady, your father is ill and asking for you," he said nervously.

Pellea reacted immediately. "My father! Oh, I must go."

Monte stopped her for only a moment. "I'll meet you at your father's room as soon as I can make it," he told her.

She nodded, her eyes wide and anxious. "I must go," she muttered distractedly, and she hurried away.

Monte looked back at the task at hand and gritted his teeth. It wasn't going to be a pretty chore, but it had to be done.

"Let's get him out of here," he said, hoisting Leonardo up with the assistance of two other men. And, just as they heard Georges arrive at the main ballroom entrance, they slipped out the side door.

"I'll be back, Georges," Monte whispered under his breath. "Get ready. We've got business between us to settle. Old business."

Monte slipped into Pellea's father's room and folded his form between the drapes to keep from being seen. Pellea was talking to the doctor and her father seemed to be sleeping.

The doctor began to pack his black bag and Pellea went to her father's bedside. Monte watched and saw the anguished love in her face as she leaned over the man. There was no denying this simple truth—she adored her father and she wouldn't leave him.

Monte closed his eyes for a moment, letting that sink in. There was no way he would be able to take her with him. All his kidnapping plans—in the dust. In order to get her to leave he would have to render her unconscious and drag her off, and that wasn't going to happen.

When the idea had first formed, he'd assumed she would come at least semi-willingly. Now he knew that was a fantasy. Her love for her father was palpable. She would never leave while he was still alive. And yet, how could he leave her behind? How could he leave her to the tender mercies of the Granvillis? The more he saw of her, the more he got to know her, the more he felt a special connection, something he'd never felt with a woman before. He wanted her with him.

But more than that, he wanted her safe. Leaving her here with Leonardo would be torture. But what could he do?

Invade, a voice deep in his soul said urgently. *The sooner the better.*

Yes. There really was no other option left.

So he would return to the continent empty-handed. Not quite what he'd promised his supporters waiting for him in Italy.

But all was not lost on that score. He had another plan—something new. Instead of kidnapping their most desirable woman, he would take their most valuable possession.

He was going to steal the tiara.

"Please tell me how he really is," she said anxiously to the doctor. "Don't sugarcoat anything. I need to know the truth." She took a deep breath and asked, "Is he in danger?"

"In other words, is he going to die tonight?" Dr. Dracken translated. "Not likely. Don't worry. But he is very weak. His heart is not keeping up as it should." He hesitated, then added, "If you really want me to be blunt, I'd have to say I wouldn't give him much more than six months. But this sort of thing is hugely unpredictable. Next year at this time, you might be chiding me for being so pessimistic."

"Oh, I hope so," she said fervently as she accompanied him to the door. "Please, do anything for him that you can think of."

"Of course. That's my job, Pellea, and I do the best I can."

The doctor left and Monte reached out and touched her as she came back into the room.

"Oh!" She jumped back, then put her hand over her heart when she realized it was him. "Monte! You scared me."

"Sorry, but once I was in, I was going to startle you no matter how I approached it."

She looked at him with tragic eyes. "My father..." Her face crumpled and she went straight into his arms and clung to him.

"Yes," he said, holding her tenderly, stroking her hair. "I heard what the doctor said. I'm so sorry, Pellea. I truly am."

She nodded. She believed him.

"He's sleeping now. The doctor gave him something. But a little while ago he was just ranting, not himself at all." She looked up into his face. "They are bringing in a nurse to stay with him tonight and tomorrow I'm going to sit with him all day."

He nodded, and then he frowned, realizing his fingers were tangling in her loosened hair. She was wearing it down. All the fancy work Magda had put into her coiffure was gone with the wind.

"Pellea, what happened to the tiara?" he asked.

She drew back and reached up as though she'd forgotten it was gone. "The guards took it back to its museum case," she said. She shook her head sadly. "I wonder if I'll ever get to wear it again."

He scowled, regretting that he'd let her get away before doing what he'd planned to do. Unfortunately, this threw a spanner into the works. Oh, he was still going to steal the thing. But now he was afraid he would have to do some actual breaking and entering in order to achieve his objective.

But when he looked at her again, he found her studying him critically, looking him up and down, admiring the uniform, and the man wearing it. He'd lost the mask somewhere, but for the rest, he looked as fresh as he had at the beginning of the evening.

"You know what?" she said at last, her head to the side, her eyes sparkling. "You would make one incredibly attractive Ambrian king."

He laughed and pulled her back into his arms, kissing her soundly. Her arms came up and circled his neck, and she kissed him back. Their bodies seemed to meet and fit together perfectly. He had a quick, fleeting thought that this might be what heaven was made of, but it was over all too soon.

She checked that her father was sleeping peacefully, then turned to Monte again. "Come sit down and wait with me," she said, pulling him by the hand. "And tell me what happened in the ballroom after I left. Did the General actually appear?"

He shook his head. "I didn't stay any longer than you did. With all the chaos that ensued upon Leonardo's... shall we call it a fall from grace...?"

He flashed her a quick grin, but she frowned in response and he sobered quickly, looking abashed.

"There you were, rushing off to see to your father. People were shouting. No one knew exactly what was going on for quite some time. And I and all my new mates picked up your fiancé and carried him to his rooms."

"I'm glad you did that," she said. "I would hate to think of what would have happened if his father had seen him like that."

"Yes," he said a bit doubtfully. "Well, we tucked him into his bed and I nosed around a little."

"Oh?"

"And I find I need to warn you of something."

She smiled. "You warning me? That's a twist on an old theme, isn't it?"

"I'm quite serious, Pellea." He hesitated until he had her complete attention. "Did it ever occur to you that you might not be the only one with a video monitoring system in this castle?"

She shrugged. "Of course. There's the main security center. Everyone knows that."

"Indeed." He gave her a significant look. "And then there's the smaller panel of screens I found in a small room off Leonardo's bedroom suite. The one that includes a crystal-clear view of your entryway."

Her eyes widened in shock. "What?"

He nodded. "I thought that might surprise you. He can see everyone who is coming in to see you, as well as when you leave."

She blanched, thinking back over what she'd done and who she'd been with in the recent past. "But not..." She looked at him sideways and swallowed hard.

"Your bedroom?" He couldn't help but smile at her reaction. "No. I didn't see any evidence of that."

"Thank God." But her relief was short-lived as she began to realize fully the implications of this news.

She frowned. "But how is it monitored? I mean...did he see you when you arrived? Or any of the other times you've come and gone?"

"I'm sure he doesn't spend most of his time sitting in front of the monitor, any more than you do."

"It would only take once."

"True."

"And how about when you arrived this time?"

Monte hesitated, then shrugged and shook his head. "I didn't come in through your entryway."

She stared at him, reminded that his mode of entering the castle was still a mystery. But for him to say flat-out that he didn't use the door—that was something of a revelation. "Then how...?"

He waved it away. "Never mind."

"But, Monte, I do mind. I want to know. How do

you get into my courtyard if you don't come in the way everyone else does?"

"I'm sorry, Pellea. I'm not going to tell you."

She frowned, not liking that at all. "You do realize that this leaves me in jeopardy of having you arrive at any inopportune moment and me not able to do anything about it."

He'd said it before and now he said it again. "I would never do anything to hurt you."

"No." She shook her head, her eyes deeply troubled. "No, Monte. That's not good enough."

He shrugged. He understood how she felt and sympathized. But what could he do? It was something he couldn't tell anyone about.

"It will have to do. I'm sorry, Pellea. I can't give away my advantage on this score. It has nothing to do with you. It has everything to do with my ability to take this country back when the time comes."

She searched his eyes, and finally gave up on the point. But she didn't like it at all. Still, the fact that Leonardo was secretly watching who came to her door was a more immediate outrage.

"Oh, I just can't believe he's watching my entry-way!"

Monte grinned. "Why are you so upset? After all, you're watching pretty much everyone in the castle yourself."

"Yes, but I'm just watching general walkways, not private entrances."

"Ah, yes," he teased. "That makes all the difference."

"It does. I wouldn't dream of setting up a monitor on Leonardo's gate."

He raised one eyebrow wisely. "Yes, but you're not interested in him. And he is very interested in you."

She thought about that for a few seconds and made a face. "I'm going to find his camera and tape it up," she vowed.

He looked pained. "Don't do that. Then he'll know you're on to him and he'll just find another way to watch you, and you might like that even less. The fact that you know about the camera gives you the advantage now. You can avoid it when you need to."

She sighed. "You're probably right," she said regretfully. It would have felt good taping over his window into her world.

There was a strange gurgling sound and they both turned to see Pellea's father rising up against his pillows.

"Father!" she cried, running to his side. "Don't try to sit up. Let me help you."

But he wasn't looking at his daughter. It was Monte he had in his sights.

"Your Majesty," he groaned painfully. "Your Royal Highness, King of Ambria."

Monte rose and faced him, hoping he would realize the man standing in his bedroom was not the king he'd served all those years ago, but that king's son. This was the first time anyone had mistaken him for his father. He felt a strange mix of honor and repulsion over it.

"My liege," Pellea's father cried, slurring his words. His thin, aged face was still handsome and his silver hair still as carefully groomed and distinguished as ever. "Wait, don't go. I need to tell you. I need to explain. It wasn't supposed to happen that way. I…I didn't mean for it to be like that."

"Father," Pellea said, trying to calm him. "Please, lie back down. Don't try to talk. Just rest."

"Don't you see?" he went on passionately, ignoring her and talking directly to the man he thought was King Grandor. "They had promised, they'd sworn you would be treated with respect. And your queen, the beautiful Elineas. No one should have touched her. It was a travesty and I swear it cursed our enterprise from the beginning."

Monte stood frozen to the spot. He heard the old man's words and they pierced his heart. It was obvious he had a message he'd been waiting a long time to deliver to Monte's father. Well, he was about twenty-five years too late.

He slid down into his covers again, now babbling almost incoherently. Pellea looked up with tears in her eyes.

"He doesn't know what he's saying," she said. "Please go, Monte. You're only upsetting him. I'll stay until the nurse comes."

Monte turned and did as she asked. His emotions were churning. He knew Pellea's father was trying to make amends of sorts, but it was a little too late. Still, it was good that he recognized that wrong had been done.

Wrong that still had to be avenged.

CHAPTER EIGHT

KNOWING PELLEA WOULD BE BUSY with her father for some time, Monte made a decision. He planned to make a visit to General Georges. Why not do it now?

A deadly calm came over him as he prepared to go. This meeting with the most evil man in his country's history was something he'd gone over a thousand times in his mind and each time there had been a different scenario, a different outcome. Which one would he choose? It didn't matter, really. They all ended up with the General mortally wounded or already dead.

The fact that his own survival might be in doubt in such an encounter he barely acknowledged and didn't worry about at all. His destiny was already set and included a confrontation with the General. That was just the way it had to be.

He strode down the hallways with confidence. He knew where the cameras were and he avoided them with ease. One of Leonardo's compadres had pointed out the General's suite to him as they'd carried Leonardo past it, and he went there now.

Breaking into the room was a simple matter. There

were no guards and the lock was a basic one. He'd learned this sort of thing as a teenager and it had stood him in good stead many times over the years.

Quietly, he slipped into the darkened room. He could hear the General snoring, and he went directly into his bedroom and yanked back the covers on his bed, ready to counter any move the older man made, whether he pulled out a gun or a cell phone.

But the man didn't move. He slept on. He seemed to have none of the effete elegance his son wore so proudly. Instead, he was large and heavy-set, but strangely amorphous, like a sculpture that had begun to melt back into a lump of clay.

"Wake up," Monte ordered. "I want to talk to you."

No response. Monte moved closer and touched the dictator. Nothing changed.

He glanced at the things on the bedside table. Bottles of fluid and a box of hypodermic needles sat waiting. His heart sank and he turned on the light and looked at the General again.

His eyes were open. He was awake.

The man was drugged. He lay, staring into space, a mere burnt-out shell of the human being he had once been. There wasn't much left. Monte realized that he could easily pick up a pillow and put it over the General's face…and that would be that. It would be a cinch. No problem at all. There wasn't an ounce of fight left in his enemy.

He stood staring down at the General for a long, long time and finally had to admit that he couldn't do it. He'd always thought he would kill Georges Granvilli if he found him. But now that he'd come face to face with him, he knew there was nothing left to kill. The man who had murdered his parents and destroyed his family was gone. This thing that was left was hardly even human.

Killing Georges Granvilli wouldn't make anything any better. He would just be a killer himself if he did it. He wasn't worth killing. The entire situation wasn't worth pursuing.

Slowly, Monte walked away in disgust.

He got back to the courtyard just moments before Pellea arrived. He thought about telling her where he'd been and what he'd seen, but he decided against it. There was no point in putting more ugliness in her thoughts right now. He could at least spare her that.

He was sitting by the fountain in the twilight atmosphere created by all the tiny fairy lights in her shrubbery when she came hurrying in through the gate.

"Monte?" she asked softly, then came straight for him like a swooping bird. As she reached him, she seized his face in her hands and kissed him on the lips, hard.

"You've got to go," she said urgently, tears in her eyes. "Go now, quickly, before they come for you."

"What have you heard?" he asked her, reaching to pull her down into his lap so that he could kiss her sweet lips once more.

"It's not what I've heard," she told him, snuggling in closely. "It's what I know. It's only logic. When all this chaos dies down and they begin to put two and two together, they'll come straight here looking for you. And you know what they'll find."

He searched her dark eyes, loving the way her long lashes made soft shadows on her cheeks. "Then we'd better get the heck out of here," he said calmly.

"No." She shook her head and looked away. "You're going. I'm staying."

He grimaced, afraid she still didn't understand the consequences of staying. "How can I leave you behind to pick up the pieces?"

"You have to go," she told him earnestly. She turned back to look at him, then reached up to run her fingers across the roughness of his barely visible beard, as though she just couldn't help herself. "When Leonardo wakes up, he's going to start asking around and trying to find out just who that man at the ball was. He'll want to know all about you and where you've been staying. And this time, they won't leave my chambers alone. They'll search with a fine-tooth comb and any evidence that you've been here will be…"

Her voice trailed off as she began to face the unavoidable fact that she was in as much danger as he was. She looked at him, eyes wide.

He was just thinking the same thing. It was torture to imagine leaving her behind. He'd turned and twisted every angle in his mind, trying to think of some way out, but the more he agonized, the more he knew there was no good answer. Unless she just gave up this obsession with staying with her father, what could he do to make sure she was protected while he was gone?

Nothing. Nothing at all.

He did have one idea, but he rejected it right away. And yet, it kept nagging at him. What if he showed her the tunnel to the outside? Then, if she was threatened, she could use it to escape.

They were bound to come after her, and even if they couldn't find any solid evidence of her ties to him, they would have their suspicions. Luckily her position and the fact that her father was so highly placed in the hierarchy would mean the most they would do at first was place her under house surveillance—meaning she would be confined to her chambers. But if her father died, or Leonardo became insanely jealous, or something else happened, all that might fall apart. In that case, it would be important for her to have a way to escape that others didn't know about. That was what made it so tempting to give her the information she needed.

Still, it was crazy even to contemplate doing that. Deep down, he didn't believe she would betray him on purpose. But what if she was discovered? What if someone saw her? His ace in the hole, his secret opening back into the castle which he and his invading force would need when he returned to claim his country back would be useless. He just couldn't risk that. Could he?

"And Monte," she was saying, getting back to the subject of her thoughts. "Leonardo's father is not a nice man."

"No?" Monte thought of the burned-out hulk he'd just been visiting. "What a surprise."

"I'm serious. Leonardo has at least some redeeming qualities. His father? None."

He looked at her seriously. "And do those redeeming qualities make him into a man you can stomach marrying?"

She avoided his eyes. "Monte..."

His arms tightened around her. "You can't kiss me the way you just did and then talk about marrying Leonardo. It doesn't work, Pellea. I've told you that before and nothing's changed." He kissed her again on her mouth, once, twice, three times, with quick hunger that grew more urgent with each kiss. He pulled her up hard against his strong body, her softness molding against him in a way that could quickly drive him crazy. Burying his face in her hair, he wanted to breathe her in, wanted to merge every part of her with every part of him.

She turned in his arms, reaching up to circle his neck, arching her body into his as though she felt the same compulsion. He dropped kisses down the length of her neck and heard her make a soft moaning sound deep in her throat. That alone almost sent him over the top, and the way her small hands felt gliding under his shirt and sliding over the muscles of his back pretty much completed the effort.

He wanted her as he'd never wanted a woman before, relentlessly, fiercely, with an insatiable need that raged through him like a hurricane. He'd felt this way about her before, but he hadn't let her know. Now, for just a few moments, he let her feel it, let her have a hint of what rode just on the other side of his patience.

She could have been shocked. She could have considered his ardor a step too far and drawn back in complete rejection. But as she felt his passion overtaking him and his desire for her so manifest, she accepted it with a willingness of her own. She wanted him, too. His marriage of the emotional need for her with the physical hunger was totally in tune with her own reactions.

But this wasn't the time. Resolutely, she pushed him back before things went too far.

He accepted her lead on it, but he had to add one thing as she slipped out of his arms.

"You belong to me," he said fiercely, his hand holding the back of her head like a globe. "Leonardo can't have you."

She tried to shake her head. "I'm going to marry him," she insisted, and though her voice was mournful, she sounded determined. "I've told you that from the moment you came today. I don't know why you won't listen."

This would be so much easier if she could tell him the truth, but that was impossible. How could he understand that she needed Leonardo even more than he needed her? She was caught in a web. If she didn't marry Leonardo, she would be considered an outcast in Ambrian traditional society.

Out-of-wedlock births were not uncommon, but they were considered beyond the pale. Once you had a baby out of wedlock, you could never be prominent in society. You would always have the taint of bad behavior about you. No one would trust your judgment and everyone would slightly despise you.

It wasn't fair, but it was the way things were.

He held her in a curiously stiff manner that left her feeling distinctly uncomfortable.

"You don't love Leonardo," he said. He'd said it before, but she didn't seem to want to accept it and act upon the fact. Maybe he should say it again and keep saying it until she realized that some things were hard, basic truths that couldn't be denied or swept under the rug.

She pulled away from him and folded her arms across her chest as though she were feeling a frost.

"I hate to repeat a cliché," she said tartly, "but here goes. What's love got to do with it?"

He nodded, his face twisted cynically. "So you admit this is a royal contract sort of wedding. A business deal."

"A power deal is more like it. Our union will cement the power arrangements necessary to run this country successfully."

"And you still think he'll want you, even if he begins to suspect…"

"I told you, love isn't involved. It's a power trade, and he wants it as much as I need it."

"Need it?" He stared at her. "Why do you 'need' it?"

She closed her eyes and shook her head. "Maybe I put it a little too strongly," she said. "I just meant… Well, you know. For my father and all."

He wasn't sure he bought that. There was something else here, something she wasn't telling him. He frowned, looking at her narrowly. He found it hard to believe that she would prefer that sort of thing to a love match. But then, he hadn't offered her a love match, had he? He hadn't even offered her a permanent friendship. So who was he to complain? And yet, he had to. He had to stop this somehow.

"Okay, I see the power from Leonardo's side," he said, mulling it over. "But where do you get yours?"

She rose and swayed in front of him, anger sparking from her eyes. She didn't like being grilled this way, mostly because she didn't have any good answers.

"For someone who wants to be ruler of Ambria, you don't know much about local politics, do you?"

He turned his hands palms-up. "If you weren't such a closed society, maybe I could be a bit more in the know," he pointed out.

She considered that and nodded reluctantly. "That's a fair point. Okay, here's the deal. Over the years, there have been many factions who have—shall we say—strained under the Granvilli rule for various reasons. A large group of dissenters, called the Practicals, have been arguing that our system is archaic and needs updating. For some reason they seem to have gravitated toward my father as their symbolic leader."

Monte grunted. "That must make life a bit dodgy for your father," he noted.

"A bit. But he has been invaluable to the rulers and

they don't dare do anything to him. And anyway, the Practicals would come unglued if they did."

"Interesting."

"The Practicals look to me as well. In fact, it may just be a couple of speeches I gave last year that set them in our direction, made them think we were kindred souls. So in allying himself with me, Leonardo hopes to blunt some of that unrest."

He gazed at her in admiration and surprise. "Who knew you were a mover and a shaker?" he said.

She actually looked a bit embarrassed. "I'm not. Not really. But I do sympathize with many of their criticisms of the way things are run. Once I marry Leonardo, I hope to make some changes."

Was that it? Did she crave the power as much as her father did? Was it really all a bid for control with her? He found that hard to believe, but when she said these things, what was he to think?

He studied her for another moment, then shrugged. "That's what they all say," he muttered, mostly to himself.

She was tempted to say something biting back, but she held her tongue. There was no point in going on with this. They didn't have much more time together and there were so many other things they could be talking about.

"Have you noticed that so far, no one seems to know who you really are?" she pointed out. As long as they didn't know who he was, his freedom might be imperiled, but his life wouldn't be. And if they should somehow realize who it was they had in their clutches… She hated to think what they might do.

"No, they don't, do they?" He frowned, not totally pleased with that. "How did *you* know, anyway? From the other time, I mean."

"You told me." She smiled at him, remembering.

"Oh. Did I?" That didn't seem logical or even realistic. He never told anyone.

"Yes, right from the first." She gave him a flirtatious look. "Right after I saved you from the guards, you kissed me and then you said, 'You can tell everyone you've been kissed by the future king of Ambria. Consider yourself blessed.'"

"I said that?" He winced a bit and laughed softly. "I guess you might be right about me having something of an ego problem."

"No kidding." She made a face. "Maybe it goes with being royal or something."

"Oh, I don't know about that." After all, he hadn't blown his cover all these years—except, it seemed, with her. "I think I do pretty well. Don't you think I blend in nicely with the average Joes?"

She shook her head, though there was a hint of laughter in her eyes. "Are you crazy? No, you do not blend in, as you so colorfully put it. Look at the way you carry yourself. The arrogance. There's no humility about you."

"No humility?" He was offended. "What are you talking about? I'm probably the most humble guy you would ever meet."

She made a sound of deprecation. "A little self-awareness would go a long way here," she noted as she looked him over critically. "But I could see that from the start. It was written all over you. And yet, I didn't kick you out as I should have."

"No, you didn't." Their gazes met and held. "But we did have an awfully good weekend, didn't we?"

"Yes." She said it softly, loving him, thinking of the child they had made together. If only she could tell him about that. Would he be happy? Probably not. That was just the way things were going to be. She loved him and he felt something pretty deep for her. But that was all they were destined to have of each other. How she would love to spend the next fifty years in his arms.

If only he weren't royal and she weren't tied to this place. If only he didn't care so much about Ambria. They could have done so well together, the two of them. She could imagine them walking on a sandy beach, chasing waves, or having a picnic by a babbling brook, skipping stones in the water, or driving around France, looking at vineyards and trying to identify the grapes.

Instead, he was planning to invade her country. And that would, of necessity, kill people she cared about. How could she stand it? Why hadn't she turned him in?

"Why does it matter so much to you, Monte?" she asked at last. "Why can't you just leave things alone?"

He looked up, his eyes dark and haunted. "Because a very large wrong was done to my family. And to this country. I need to make things right again. That's all I live for."

His words stabbed into her soul like sharp knives. If this was all he lived for, what could she ever be to him?

"Isn't there someone else who could do it?" she asked softly. "Does it have to be you?"

Reaching out, he put his hand under the water raining down from the fountain. Drops bounced out and scattered across his face, but he seemed to welcome them. "I'm the crown prince. I can't let others fight my battles for me."

"But you have brothers, don't you?"

He nodded. "There were five of us that night. Or rather, seven. Five boys and twin girls." He was quiet for a moment, remembering. "I hunted for them all for years. I started once I enrolled in university in England. I studied hard, but I spent a lot of time poring over record books in obscure villages, hoping to find some clue. There was nothing."

He sighed, in his own milieu now. "Once I entered the business world and then did some work for the Foreign Office, I developed contacts all over the world. And those have just begun to pan out. As I think I told you, I've made contact with two of my brothers, the two closest to me in age. But the others are still a mystery."

"Are you still looking?"

"Of course. I'll be looking until I find them all. For the rest of my life if need be." He shrugged. "I don't know if they are alive or not. But I'll keep looking." He turned and looked at her, his eyes burning. "Once we're all together, there will be no stopping us."

She shook her head, unable to imagine how growing up without any contact with his family would have affected this young Ambrian prince.

"What was it like?" she asked him. "What happened to you as a child? It must have been terrible to grow up alone."

He nodded. "It wasn't great. I had a wonderful family until I was eight years old. After that, it was hit or miss. I stayed with people who didn't necessarily know who I was, but who knew I had to be hidden. I ended up with a couple who were kind to me but hardly loving." He shrugged. "Not that it mattered. I wasn't looking for a replacement for my mother, nor for my father. No one could replace either one of them and I didn't expect it."

"Why were they hiding you?"

"They were trying to keep the Granvillis from having me killed."

"Oh." She colored as though that were somehow her fault. "I see."

"We were all hidden. From each other, even. You understand that any surviving royals were a threat to the Granvilli rule, and I, being the crown prince, am the biggest threat of all."

"Of course. I get it."

"We traveled a lot. I went to great schools. I had the sort of upbringing you would expect of a royal child, minus the love. But I survived and in fact, I think I did pretty well."

"It wasn't until I found my brother Darius that I could reignite that family feeling and I began to come alive again. Family is everything and I had lost mine."

"And your other brother?"

"A young woman who worked for an Ambrian news agency in the U.S. found Cassius. He was only four during the coup and he didn't remember that he was royal. He'd grown up as a California surfer and spent time in the military. Finding out his place in life has been quite a culture shock to him. He's trying to learn how to be royal, but it isn't easy for a surfer boy. I only hope he can hold it all together until we retake our country."

The old wall clock struck the time and it was very late, well after midnight. She looked at him and sighed. "You must go," she told him.

He looked back at her and wondered how he could leave her here. "Come with me, Pellea," he said, his voice crackling with intensity. "Come with me tonight. By late morning, we'll be in France."

She closed her eyes. She was so tired. "You know I can't," she whispered.

He rose and came over to kiss her softly on her full, red lips. "Then come and get some sleep," he told her. "I'll go just before dawn."

"Will you wake me up when you go?" she asked groggily.

"Yes. I'll wake you."

And would he show her his escape secrets? That was

probably a step too far. He couldn't risk it. He had to think of more lives than just their two. So he promised he would wake her, but he didn't promise he would let her see him go.

She lay down in her big, fluffy bed and he lay down on her long couch, which was almost as comfortable. He didn't understand why she wouldn't let him sleep beside her. She seemed to have some strange sense of a moral duty to Leonardo. Well, if it was important to her, he wasn't going to mess with it. She had to do what she had to do, just like he did. Lying still and listening to her breathe on the bed so near and yet so far, he almost slept.

CHAPTER NINE

THE MOMENT PELLEA WOKE, she knew Monte was gone. It was still dark and nowhere near dawn, but he was gone. Just as she'd thought.

She curled into a ball of misery and wept. Someday she would have his child to console her, but right now there was nothing good and beautiful and strong and true in her life but Monte. And he was gone.

But wait. She lifted her head and thought for a moment. He'd promised to say goodbye. He wouldn't break his promise. If he didn't tell her in person, he would at least have left a note, and there was nothing. That meant…he was still somewhere in the castle.

Her heart stopped in her throat. What now? Where could he be? Dread filled her since, surely, he would get caught. He would be killed. He would have to leave without saying goodbye! She couldn't stand it. None of the above was tolerable. She had to act fast.

Rising quickly, she went to the surveillance room with the security monitors and began to study them. All looked quiet. It was about three in the morning, and she detected no movement.

Maybe she was wrong. Maybe he had gone without saying goodbye. Darn it all!

That's when she saw something moving in the museum. A form. A tall, graceful masculine form. Monte! What was he doing in the museum room?

The tiara!

She groaned. "No, Monte!" she cried, but of course he couldn't hear her.

And then, on another panel, she saw the guards. There were three of them and they were moving slowly down the hallway toward the museum, looking like men gearing up for action. There was no doubt in her mind. They'd been alerted to his presence and would nab him.

Her heart was pounding out of her chest. She had to act fast. She couldn't let them catch him like this. They would throw him in jail and Leonardo would hear of it and Monte's identity would be revealed and he would be a dead man. She groaned.

She couldn't let that happen. There was only one thing she could do. She had to go there and stop it.

In another moment she was racing through the hallways, her white nightgown billowing behind her, her hair a cloud of golden blond, and her bare feet making a soft padding sound on the carpeted floors.

She ran, heedless of camera positions, heedless of anyone who might step out and see her. Who would be watching at this time of night anyway? Only the very men she'd seen going after Monte. She had one goal and that was to save his singularly annoying life. If only she could get there in time.

The museum door was ajar. She burst in and came face to face with Monte, but he was standing before her in handcuffs, with a guard on either side. Behind them, she could see the tiara, glistening on its mount inside the glass case. At least he didn't have it in his hands.

She stared into Monte's eyes for only a second or two, long enough to note the look of chagrin he wore at being caught, and then she swung her attention onto the guards.

"What is going on here?" she demanded, her stern gaze brooking no attitude from any of them. She knew how to pour on the superior pose when she had to and she was playing it to the hilt right now. Even standing there barefoot and in her nightgown she radiated control.

The guards were wide-eyed. They knew who she was but they'd never seen her like this. After a moment of surprised reaction, the captain stepped forward.

"Miss, we have captured the intruder." He nodded toward Monte and looked quite pleased with himself.

She blinked, then gestured toward Monte with a sweep of her hand. "You call this an intruder?" she said sternly, her lip curling a bit in disdain.

"Uh." The captain looked at her and then looked away again. "We caught him red-handed, Miss. He was trying to steal the tiara. Look, you can see that the lock was forced open."

"Uh." The second in command tugged on the captain's shirt and whispered in his ear.

The captain frowned and turned back to Pellea, looking most disapproving.

"I'm told you might have been dancing with this gentleman at the ball, Miss," he said. "Perhaps you can identify him for us."

"Certainly," she said in a sprightly manner. "He's a good friend of Leonardo's."

"Oh." All three appeared shocked and Monte actually gave her a triumphant wink which she ignored as best she could. "Well, there may be something there. Mr. Leonardo, is it?"

Just his name threw them for a loop. Everyone was terrified of Leonardo. They shuffled their feet but the captain wasn't cowed.

"Still, we found him breaking into the museum case," he noted. "You can't do that."

"Is anything missing?" she asked, looking bored with it all.

"No. We caught him in time."

"Well then." She gave a grand shrug. "All's well that ends well, isn't it?"

The captain frowned. "Not exactly. I'm afraid I have to make a report of this to the General. He'll want to know the particulars and might even want to interview the intruder himself."

Not a good outcome. Monte gave her a look that reminded her that this would be a bad ending to this case. But she already knew as much.

"Oh, I doubt that," she said airily. "If you have some time to question him yourself, I think you will find the problem that is at the root of all this."

The captain frowned. He obviously wasn't sure he

liked the interference being run by this know-it-all from the regime hierarchy. "And that is?"

She sighed as though it was just so tedious to have to go over the particulars.

"My good man, it was a ball. You know how men get. This one and Leonardo were challenging each other to a drinking contest." She shrugged elaborately. "Leonardo is now out cold in his room. I'm sure you'll find this fellow..." She gestured his way. "...who you may know as the Count of Revanche, isn't in much better shape. He may not show it but he has no clue what he's doing."

The guards looked at Monte. He gave them a particularly mindless grin. They frowned as Monte added a mock fierce look for good measure. The guards glanced away and shuffled their feet again.

"Well, miss," said the captain, "What you say may be true and all. But he was still found in the museum room, and the lock was tampered with and that just isn't right."

Pellea bit her lip, biding for time. They were going to be sticklers, weren't they? She felt the need of some reinforcement. For that, she turned to Monte.

"Please, Your Highness, tell us what you were doing in the museum room."

He gave her a fish-eyed look before he turned to the guards and gave it a try.

"I was..." He managed to look a little woozy. "I was attempting to steal the tiara." He said it as though it were a grand announcement.

"What on earth!" she cried, feeling all was lost and wondering what he was up to.

"Don't you understand?" he said wistfully. "It's so beautiful. I wanted to give it back to you so that you could wear it again."

She stared at him, dumbfounded at how he could think this was a good excuse.

"To me?" she repeated softly.

"Yes. You looked enchanting in it, like a fairy-tale princess, and I thought you should have it, always." His huge, puppy-dog eyes were doing him a service, but some might call it over the top for this job.

"But, it's not mine," she reminded him sadly.

"No?" He looked a bit puzzled by that. "Well, it should be."

She turned to the guards. "You see?" she said, throwing out her hands. "He's not in his right mind. I think you should let me take him off your hands. You don't really want to bother the General with this trifle, especially at this time of night. Do you?"

The captain tried to look stern. "Well, now that you mention it, miss…"

She breathed a sigh of relief. "Good, I'll just take him along then."

They were shuffling their feet again. That seemed to be a sign that they weren't really sure what they should be doing.

"Would you like one of us to come along and help you handle him?" the captain asked, groping for his place in all this.

"No, I think he'll be all right." She took hold of his hands, bound by the handcuffs, and the captain handed her the key. "He usually does just what I tell him," she lied happily. She'd saved him. She could hardly contain her excitement.

"I see, miss. Good night, then."

"Good night, Captain. Men." She waved at them merrily and began to lead Monte away. "Come along now, Count," she murmured to him teasingly. "I've got you under house arrest. You'd better do what I tell you to from now on."

"That'll be the day," he said under his breath, but his eyes were smiling.

Once back in her courtyard, they sat side by side on the garden bench and leaned back, sighing with relief.

"You're crazy," she told him matter-of-factly. "To risk everything for a tiara."

"It's a very special tiara," he reminded her. "And by all rights, it belongs to my family."

"Maybe so, but there are others who would fight you for it," she said, half closing her eyes and thinking about getting more sleep. "You almost pulled it off," she added.

"Yes."

She turned to look at him. "And you actually seemed to know what you were doing. Why was that? Have you been moonlighting as a jewel thief or something?"

He settled back and smiled at her. "In fact, I do know what I'm doing around jewelry heists," he stated calmly.

"I apprenticed myself to a master jewel thief one summer. He taught me everything he knew."

She frowned at him for a long moment. It was late. Perhaps she hadn't heard him correctly. But did he say…?

"What in the name of common sense are you talking about?" she said, shaking her head in bewilderment. "Why would you do such a thing?"

He shrugged. "I wanted to learn all I could about breaking into reinforced and security-protected buildings. I thought it would be a handy talent to have when it came time to reassert my monarchy on this island nation."

She stared at him in wonder, not sure if she was impressed or appalled. But it did show another piece of evidence of the strength of his determination to get his country back. This was pretty obviously an ambition she wasn't going to be able to fight.

Sighing, she shook her head and turned away. "Well, maybe you should go back for a refresher course," she noted.

He raised an eyebrow. "What are you talking about?"

She looked back at him. "Well, you didn't get the tiara, did you?"

"What makes you say that?" He smiled and reached back and pulled something out of the back of his shirt and held it up to the light, where it glittered spectacularly.

"You mean this tiara?" he asked her.

She stared at it as it flashed color and fire all around the room. "But I saw it in the case in the museum."

"You saw a copy in the case." He held it even higher and looked at it, admiring its beauty. "This is the real thing."

She was once again bewildered by him. "I don't understand."

"What you saw was a replica. My grandmother had it made years ago. I remembered that my mother had it in a secret hiding place. I went over to that side of the castle and, lo and behold, I found it."

"That's amazing. After all this time? I can hardly believe it."

"Yes. It seems that most of my family's private belongings were shoved into a big empty room and have been forgotten. Luckily for me."

She shook her head. "But now that you have the tiara, what are you going to do with it?"

"Take it back with me." He tucked it away and leaned over to take her hand in his. "If I can't take their most beautiful woman from them, at least I can take their prized royal artifact." He smiled. "And when you think about it, the tiara actually belongs to me. Surely you see that."

She laced her fingers with his and yearned toward him. "You're just trying to humiliate them, aren't you? You would have preferred to do it by stealing me away, but since that's not possible, you take the tiara instead."

"Yes," he said simply. "The answer is yes."

"But…"

"Don't you understand, Pellea? I want them thrown off-center. I want them to wonder what my next move might be. I want them to doubt themselves." The spirit of the royal warrior was back in his eyes. "Because when I come back, I'm going to take this country away from them."

He sounded sure of himself, but in truth, here in the middle of the night, he was filled with misgivings and doubts. Would he really be able to restore the monarchy? Would he get his family back into the position they'd lost twenty-five years before? Night whispers attacked his confidence and he had to fight them back.

Because he had to succeed. And he would, damn it, or die trying. No doubts could be allowed. His family belonged here and they would be back. This was what his whole life had been aimed at.

It was time to go. Actually, it was way past time to go, but he had run up against the wall by now. He had to follow the rules of logic and get out of here before someone showed up at Pellea's gate. It was just a matter of time.

But there was something else. He had made a decision. He was going to show Pellea the tunnel. There was no other option. If he couldn't take her with him, he had to give her some way to escape if things got too bad.

He was well aware of what he was doing—acting like a fool under the spell of a woman. If he were watching a friend in the same circumstances, he would be yelling, "Stop!" right now. Every bit of common sense argued against it. You just didn't risk your most important advantages like that.

After all, there were so many imponderables. Could he trust her? He was sure he could, and yet, how many men had said that and come out the loser in the end? Could he really take a woman who claimed she was going to marry into the family of the enemy and expect her to keep his confidences? Was he crazy to do this? He knew he was risking everything by placing a bet on her integrity and her fidelity—a bet that could be lost so easily. How many men had been destroyed putting too much trust in love?

For some reason the lyrics to "Blues in the Night" came drifting into his head. But who took their advice from old songs, anyway?

He had to trust her, because he had to protect her. There was nothing else he could do.

"Pellea," he said, taking her into his arms. "I'm going."

"Oh, thank God!" She held his face in her hands and looked at him with all the love she possessed. "I won't rest easy until you get to Italy."

He kissed her softly. "But I need you to do me a favor."

"Anything."

He was looking very serious. "I want you to keep a secret."

She smiled. "Another one?"

He touched her face and winced, as though she was

almost too beautiful to bear. "I'm going to show you how I get into the castle."

Her face lost its humor and went totally still. She understood right away how drastic this was for him. He'd refused even to hint at this to her all along. Now he was going to show her the one ace in the hole he had—the chink in the castle's armor. Her heart began to beat a bit faster. She knew very well that this was a heavy responsibility.

"All right," she said quietly. "And Monte, please don't worry. I will never, ever show this to anyone."

He looked at her and loved her, loved her noble face, loved her noble intentions. He knew she meant that with all her heart and soul, but he also knew that circumstances could change. Stranger things had happened. Still, he had to do it. He couldn't live with himself if he didn't leave behind some sort of escape route for her.

He frowned, thinking of what he was doing. It wouldn't be enough to show her where it was. The tunnel was old and dark and scary. He remembered when he'd first tried to negotiate it a few weeks before. He'd always known about it—it was the way he and his brothers had escaped on that terrible night all those years ago. And it had been immediately obvious no one had used it since. That was the benefit of having strangers take over your castle. If they made themselves hateful enough, no one would tell them the castle secrets.

When he'd come through, in order to pass he'd had to cut aside huge roots which had grown in through cracks. For someone like Pellea, it might be almost impassable.

It would be better if she came partway with him so that she would see what it was like and wouldn't be intimidated by the unknown.

"Bring a flashlight," he told her. "You're going to need it."

She followed him. He took her behind the fountain, behind the clump of ancient shrubs that seemed to grow right out of the rocks. He moved some smaller stones, then pushed aside a boulder that was actually made of pumice and was much lighter than it looked. And there, just underfoot, was a set of crumbling steps and a dank, dark tunnel that spiraled down.

"Here it is," he told her. "Think you can manage it?"

She looked down. It would be full of spiders and insects and slimy moss and things that would make her scream if she saw them. But she swallowed hard and nodded.

"Of course," she said, trying hard to sound nonchalant. "Let's go."

He showed her how to fill in the opening behind her, and then they started off. And it was just as unpleasant a journey as she'd suspected it would be. In twenty-five years, lots of steps had crumbled and roots had torn apart some walls. The natural breakdown of age was continuing apace and wouldn't be reversed until someone began maintaining the passageway. Even with a flashlight, the trip was dark and foreboding and she was glad she had Monte with her.

"Just ahead there is a small window," he told her. "We'll stop there and you can go back."

"All right," she said, shuddering to think what it was going to be like when she was alone.

"How are you feeling?" he said.

"Nauseated," she said before she thought. "But I'm always sick in the morning lately."

As soon as the words were past her lips she regretted them. How was it that she could feel so free and open to saying anything that came into her head when she was with him? And then she ended up saying too much. She glanced at him, wondering if he'd noticed.

He gave no sign of it. He helped her down the last set of stairs and there was the thin slit of a window, just beginning to show the dawn coming out over the ocean. They stopped and sat to rest. He pulled her close, tightening his arm around her and kissing her cheek.

She turned her face to accept his lips and he gave her more. Startled, she found in the heat of his mouth a quick arousal, calling up a passionate response from her that would have shocked her if she hadn't already admitted to herself that this man was all she ever wanted, body and soul. She drew back, breathless, heart racing and he groaned as she turned away.

"Pellea, you can't marry Leonardo. I don't care how much your father wants you to. It won't end up the way he hopes anyway. Nothing like that ever does. You can't sell your soul for security. It doesn't work."

"Monte, you don't really know everything. And you can't orchestrate things from afar. I've got to deal with the hand I've been dealt. You won't be here and you won't figure in. That's just the way it has to be."

"You don't understand. This is different. I'm making you a promise." He hesitated, steeling himself for what he had to do. "I'm going to move up operations. We'll invade by midsummer. I'll come and get you." He brushed the loose curls back from her face and looked at her with loving intensity. Here in the gloom, she was like a shining beacon in the dark.

"Leonardo's brand of protection won't do you any good by then. I'll be the one your father will have to look to."

His words struck fear into her heart. She turned, imploring him.

"No, Monte. You can't do that. You'll put yourself and all your men in danger if you try to come before your forces are ready. You can't risk everything just for me." She reached up and grabbed the front of his shirt in both hands. "I can't let you do that."

He gazed back steadily. "We'll have right and emotion on our side. We'll win anyway."

"Monte, don't be crazy. You know life doesn't work like that. Just being right, or good, or the nicest, doesn't win you a war. You need training and equipment and the manpower and..."

He was laughing at her and she stopped, nonplussed. "What is it?"

"You sound as though you've taken an army into the field yourself," he told her. "If I didn't know better, I would think you were a natural-born queen."

She flushed, not sure whether he was making fun of her. "I only know I want you safe," she said, her voice trembling a bit.

He took her into his arms. "I'll be safe. You're the one who needs protecting. You're the one ready to put your trust in the Granvillis."

She shook her head. "It's not like that," she said, but he wasn't listening.

He gazed at her, his blue eyes troubled. "I'll do anything I have to do to keep you from harm."

"You can't do it. You can't invade until you're ready."

"We'll get ready." He lifted her chin with his finger. "Just don't ruin everything by marrying Leonardo."

She turned away. Another wave of nausea was turning her breathless.

"What is it?" he said.

She shook her head. "I'm…I'm just a little sick."

He sat back a moment, watching her. "Have you been having that a lot lately?"

She couldn't deny it. She looked up and tried to make a joke out of it. "Yes. I imagine the situation in the world brings on nausea in most sane people at least once a day."

He frowned. "Possibly." A few bits of scattered elements came together and formed a thought. He remembered the way she seemed to want to protect her belly. The book at her bedside. The sudden aversion to alcohol. "Or maybe you're pregnant."

She went very still.

"Are you, Pellea? Are you pregnant?"

She paled, then tried to answer, but no words came out of her mouth.

"You are."

Suddenly the entire picture cleared for him. Of course. That explained everything—the reluctance to recreate the love they'd shared, the hurry to get him out of her hair, the rush to marry Leonardo. But something else was also clear. If she was pregnant, he had no doubt at all that the baby was his.

What the hell!

"You're pregnant with my baby and you weren't going to tell me about it?"

Outrage filled his voice and generated from his body. He shook his head, unable to understand how she could have done this. "And you plan to marry Leonardo?" he added in disbelief.

That rocked him back on his heels. He couldn't accept these things. They made no sense.

"Pellea…" He shook his head, unable to find the words to express how devastated he was…and angry.

She turned on him defensively. "I have to marry *some-one*," she said crisply. "And you aren't going to marry me, are you?"

She held her breath, waiting for his response to that one, hoping beyond all logic.

He stared at her, rage mixing with confusion. He couldn't marry her. Could he? But if she was carry-ing his child… This was something new, something he hadn't even considered. Did it change everything? Or was everything already set in stone and unchangeable?

He turned away, staring out at the ocean through the tiny window in the wall. She waited and watched the emotions crossing in his face and knew he wrestled with his feelings for her, his brand-new feelings for his child, and his role as the crown prince and a warrior king. He was torn, unprepared for such big questions all at once. She had to give him a bit of space. But she'd hoped for more. It wasn't like him to be so indecisive.

And, as he didn't seem to be able to find words that would heal things between them, her heart began to sink. What was the use of him telling her that they had to be together if he wasn't prepared to take the steps that might lead to something real? If he would never even consider making her his wife?

He had a lot of pride as the royal heir to Ambria. Well, she had a bit of pride herself. And she wasn't going anywhere without a promise of official status. If she wasn't good enough to marry, she would find another way to raise her child.

He turned back, eyes hard and cold as ice. "You have to come with me," he said flatly.

She was already shaking her head. "You know I can't go with you while my father lives."

Frustration filled his face and he turned away again, swearing softly. "I know," he said at last, his hands balled into fists. "And I can't ask you to abandon him."

"Never."

"But, Pellea, you have to listen…"

Whatever he was about to say was lost to history. An alarm went off like a bomb, echoing against the walls of the castle, shaking it to its foundations. They turned, reaching for each other, and then clinging together as the walls seemed to shake.

He looked questioningly at her. "What is it?" he asked her roughly.

"The castle alarm," she said. "Something must have happened. I haven't heard an alarm like this since…since Leonardo's mother died."

He stepped back, listening. "I thought for a moment it was an earthquake," he muttered, frowning. "Do you think…?"

"I don't know," she said, answering his unspoken question.

The alarm continued to sound. Pellea put her hands over her ears.

And just as suddenly as it had begun, it stopped. They stared at each other for a long moment.

"I'm going back," she said.

He nodded. He'd known she would. He had never wanted anything more strongly than he wanted her to come with him and yet he knew she couldn't do it. He was sunk in misery such as he'd never known before— misery in his own inability to control things. Misery in leaving behind all that he loved. And even the concept of a new baby that he would take some time to deal with.

"One more thing," he noted quickly. "Come here to the window." He waited while she positioned herself to look out. "Listen to me carefully. When you escape, wait until you get out into the sunlight, then look out across that wide, mowed field and you will see a small cottage that looks like something left over from a fairy tale. Go directly to it, ask for Jacob. I'll warn him that you may be coming. He will take you to the boat that will transfer you to the continent."

"If I escape," she amended softly, feeling hopeless.

He grasped her by the shoulders. "You will. One way or another, you will. And when you do, you'll come to me. Do you swear it?"

She nodded, eyes filling with tears.

"Say the words," he ordered.

"I swear I'll come to you," she said, looking up through her tears.

He stared into her eyes for a long moment, then kissed her.

"Goodbye," she said, pulling away and starting up the steps. "Good luck." She looked back and gave him a watery smile. "Until Ambria is free," she said, throwing him a kiss.

"Until Ambria is free," he saluted back. "I love you, Pellea," he called after her as she disappeared up the stairs. "And I love our baby," he whispered, but only to himself.

He would be back. He would come to claim what was his, in every way, or die trying. Cursing, he began to race down the stairs.

CHAPTER TEN

PELLEA GOT BACK without anyone knowing that she'd been gone and she covered up the escape tunnel exactly as Monte had in the past. She didn't find out what the alarm had been about until Kimmee came by with her breakfast.

"I guess the old General is really sick," she said, slightly in awe. "Can you believe it? I thought that man would be immortal. Anyway, someone went in to give him his morning coffee and thought he was dead. So they set off the alarm. Leonardo is furious."

"But he's not really dead."

"Not yet. But they say he's not far from it."

Despite everything, Pellea was upset. "How sad to come all this way home after all this time without really having a chance to see anyone he cares for," she said.

"Maybe," Kimmee said. "Or maybe," she whispered, leaning close, "the meanness finally caught up with him."

"Don't speak that way of the sick," Pellea said automatically, but inside, she agreed.

Still, she had a hard time dwelling on the sad condition

of the man who had been Ambria's leader for all her life. Mostly, she was thinking about Monte and his pledge to invade very soon, and she was sick at heart. She knew what danger he would be putting himself and his men in if he invaded now. If he did this just because of her and he was hurt—if anyone was hurt—she would never forgive herself.

Leonardo came by before noon. She went to meet him at the gate with her heart in her throat, wondering what he knew and what he was going to suspect. He looked like a man seriously hung-over and rather distracted by his current situation, but other than that, he seemed calm enough.

"Hello, my dear," he said. "I'm sure you've heard about my father."

"Yes. Leonardo, I'm so sorry."

"Of course, but it's not unexpected. He's been quite ill, you know. A lot worse than we'd told the people. It's a natural decline, I suppose. But for that moron to start the alarm as though he were dead!" He shook his head. "I've dealt with him." He slapped his gloves against his pant leg and looked at her sideways. "That was quite a night we had, wasn't it? I'm afraid we never did get around to announcing our engagement, did we?"

She realized he was asking her, as though he wasn't quite sure what had happened the night before. What on earth would she tell him? Nothing. That was by far the wisest course.

"No, we didn't," she said simply.

He studied her face. "Does that mean that the wedding is off?" he asked musingly.

She hesitated, not really sure what he wanted from her. "What do you think?" she asked him.

He made a face. "I think there was someone at the ball who you would rather marry," he said bluntly.

"Oh, Leonardo," she began.

But he cut her off. "Never mind, darling. We'll have to deal with this later. Right now I've got my hands full. I've got my father's ill health to come to terms with. And then there are the plans for succession."

"Why? What's going on?"

"You haven't heard?"

"No. Tell me."

"You know that my father arrived last night. They brought him in from France. I hadn't seen him for weeks. I didn't realize…" He stopped and rubbed his eyes. "My father is a vegetable, Pellea. I'm going to have to file for full custodial rights. And every little faction in the castle is sharpening its little teeth getting ready to try to grab its own piece of power." He shook his head. "It's a nightmare."

"Oh, Leonardo, I'm so sorry."

"Yes. It's all on me now, my sweet. I don't know if I have time for a marriage. Sorry."

Leonardo shrugged and turned to leave, his mind on other things. Pellea watched him go and sighed with relief. That was one hurdle she wasn't going to have to challenge at any rate.

Not that it left her in the clear. She was still pregnant.

She was still without a husband. What would become of her and her baby? She closed her eyes, took a deep breath and forced herself to focus. She had to think. It was time to find some new answers.

Pellea went to sit with her father later that day. He was much better. She wasn't sure what the doctor had given him, but she could see that his mind was clear once again and she was grateful.

She chatted with him for a few minutes and then he surprised her with a pointed question.

"Who was that man who was here yesterday?" he asked.

"The doctor?" she tried evasively.

"No. The other man. The one I momentarily mistook for King Grandor."

She took in a deep breath. "It was his son, the crown prince. It was Monte DeAngelis."

"Monte?" He almost smiled. "Oh, yes, of course it was Monte. I remember him well. A fine, strapping lad he was, too." He shook his head. "I'm so glad to see that he survived."

She paused, then decided to let honesty rule the day. "He makes a pretty good grown man as well," she said quietly.

"Yes." His gaze flickered up to smile at her. "I saw him kissing you."

"Oh." It seemed her father hadn't been as out of it as she had supposed. Well, good. He might as well know the truth. Did she have the nerve to go on with the honesty? Why not? What did she have to lose at this point?

"I'm in love with him, Father. And I'm carrying his child."

There. What more was there to say? She waited, holding her breath.

He closed his eyes and for a moment she was afraid what she'd said was too much for him.

"I'm so sorry, Father," she said, leaning over him. "Please forgive me."

"There's nothing to forgive," he said, opening his eyes and smiling at her. "Not for you at any rate. I would assume this is going to put an end to my plans for you to marry Leonardo."

She shook her head, sorry to disappoint him. "I'm afraid so."

He frowned. "The powers that be won't like it."

"No."

For the next few minutes he was lost in thought. She tidied things in the room and got him a fresh bottle of water. And finally, he took her hand and told her what he wanted to do next.

"I'd like to see the doctor," he said, his voice weak but steady. "I think we'd better make some plans. I'm about to leave this life, but I want to do something for you before I go."

"No, Father, you don't have to do anything more for me. You've done everything for me my whole life. It's enough. Just be well and stay alive for as long as you can. I need you."

He patted her hand. "That is why I need the doctor. Please see if you can get him right away."

She drew in her breath, worried. "I'll go right now."

The doctor came readily enough. He'd always been partial to Pellea and her father. After he talked to the older man, he nodded and said, "I'll see if I can pull some strings."

"Good," her father said once he was gone. "Leonardo will have his work cut out for him fighting off all the factions that will try to topple his new rule. He doesn't have time to think about me. I'm of no use to him now anyway and in no condition to help him." He took his daughter's hand in his and smiled at her. "The doctor will get me permission to go to the continent to see a specialist. And I'll need you to go along as one of my nurses."

"What?" She could hardly believe her ears. They were going to the continent. Just like that. Could it really be this easy?

"Are you willing?" he asked her.

"Oh, Father!" Pellea's eyes filled with tears and her voice was choked. "Father, you are saving my life."

Arriving in Italy two days later, Pellea was more nervous than ever. She wanted to see Monte again, but she was afraid of what she would find when she did. After all, how many times and in how many ways had he told her that he would never marry her? She knew there wasn't much hope along those lines.

And there was more. She knew very well that the

excitement of a clandestine affair was one thing. The reality of a pregnant woman knocking on the door was another. He might very well have decided she wasn't worth the effort by the time he got home. Was that possible? She didn't like to think so, but reality could be harsh and cold.

Still, one thing was certain. She had to go to him. She had to let him know that she was not in danger any longer, that she was not marrying Leonardo, and that her well-being was not a reason to launch an invasion. She was no longer in Ambria and no longer in need of any sort of rescue. The last thing in the world she wanted was to be the catalyst for a lot of needless killing.

She'd left her father in a clinic in Rome and she'd traveled a few hours into the mountains to the little town of Piasa where she knew Ambrian ex-patriots tended to gather. She found his hotel, and with heart beating wildly, she went to the desk and asked for him.

"He's not seeing visitors, miss," the concierge told her. "Perhaps if you left your name…"

How could she leave her name? She wasn't staying anywhere he would be able to find her. She turned away from the hotel desk in despair, losing hope, wondering where she could go.

And then, there he was, coming out of an elevator with two other men, laughing at something someone had said. Joy surged in her heart, but so did fear, and when he looked up and saw her, her heart fell. He didn't look happy to see her. He seemed almost annoyed.

He excused himself from the other men and came

toward her. He didn't smile. Instead, he pressed a room key into her hand.

"Go to room twenty-five and wait for me," he told her softly. Then he turned on his heel and went back to the men, immediately cracking a joke that made them laugh uproariously, one even glancing back at where she stood. Had he told them why she was here? Was he making fun of her? Her cheeks flamed crimson and, for just a moment, she was tempted to throw the key in his face and storm out.

Luckily, she calmed down quickly. There was no way she could know what he'd said to the other men, or even what he was thinking. He might have needed some sort of ruse to maintain his situation. She had no way of knowing and it would be stupid of her to make assumptions. Taking a deep breath, she headed for the elevator.

She found her way to the room, and despite her sensible actions, she was still numb with shock at the way he'd acted. Just as she'd feared, he was another person entirely when he wasn't in the castle of Ambria. What was next? Was he going to hand her money to get lost? And if he did that, how would she respond? She was sick at heart. This wasn't what she'd hoped for.

She paced the room for a few minutes, but she was so tired. After a few longing looks at his bed, she gave in to temptation and lay down for a rest. Very quickly, she fell asleep.

But not for long. The next thing she knew, someone was lying next to her on the bed and kissing her ear.

"Oh!" she said, trying to get up.

But it was no use. Monte was raining down kisses all over her and she began to laugh.

"What are you doing?"

"Some people welcome with flowers," he told her with a sweet, slow grin. "I do it with kisses. Now lie still and take it like a woman."

She giggled as he dropped even more kisses on her. "Monte! Cut it out. I'm going to get hysterical."

"Do you promise?"

"No! I mean… Oh, you know what I mean."

He did, and he finally stopped, but his hand was covering her belly. "Boy or girl?" he asked her softly.

She smiled up at him, happiness tingling from every inch of her. "I don't know yet."

"It's hard to believe."

She nodded. "Just another miracle," she said. "Are you happy about it?"

He stared into her eyes for a long moment before answering, and she was starting to worry about just what his answer was going to be, when he spoke.

"*Happy* isn't a strong enough word," he told her simply. "I feel something so strong and new, I don't know what the word is. But there's a balloon of wonderfulness in my chest and it keeps getting bigger and bigger. It's as though a new world has opened at my feet." He shrugged. "And now that you're here, everything is good."

She sighed. "I was worried. The way you looked when you saw me…"

"In public you'll find I am one person, Pellea. In

private, quite another. It's a necessary evil that someone in my position has to be so careful all the time." He traced her lips with his finger. "But with you, I promise always to be genuine. You'll always know the real me, good or bad."

She was listening, and it was all very nice, but she still hadn't heard certain words she was waiting for. She told him about what had happened at the castle, and how she had accompanied her father for his visit to the specialist.

"I hope they can do something for him," she said.

"Does he plan to go back?"

"Oh, I'm sure he does. His life is in Ambria."

He nodded thoughtfully. "You're not going back," he said, as though he had the last word in the decision.

"Really?" She raised an eyebrow. "And just what is going to keep me here?"

"I am."

She waited. There should be more to that statement. But he frowned as though he was thinking about something else. She was losing her patience.

"I've got to get back to my father," she said, rising from the bed and straightening her clothing.

Monte rose as well. "I'm going with you," he said firmly.

She looked up at him in surprise. "But…you hate him."

"No." He shook his head. "I hate the man he used to be. I don't hate the man he is today."

"You think he's changed?"

"I think we all have." He pulled her close. "And anyway, there are no good jewelers here in Piasa. I need to go to Rome. I need a larger city to find a real artist."

"Why would you want a jeweler?"

"I need a good copy made."

"Of the tiara?" She scrunched up her face, trying to figure out what he would want that for.

"In a way. I'd like to find someone who could reproduce the main part of the tiara as…" He smiled at her. "…as an engagement ring."

Her eyes widened. "Oh."

He kissed her on the mouth. "Would you wear a ring like that?"

And suddenly she felt as though she were floating on a cloud of happiness. "I don't know. It would depend on who gave it to me."

"Good answer." And he kissed her again, then took her two hands in his and smiled down at her. "I love you, Pellea," he said, his feelings shining in his eyes. "My love for you is bigger than revenge, bigger than retribution, bigger than the wounds of the past. I'm going to take care of all those things in good time. I'm going to get my country back. And when I take over, I want you with me, as my queen. Will you be my wife?"

She drew in a full breath of air and laughed aloud. There they were. Those were the words she'd been waiting for.

"Yes, Monte," she said, reaching for the man she loved, joy surging in her. "With all my heart and soul."

✦ Harlequin® *Romance*

Coming Next Month

Available February 8, 2011

BABIES AND BRIDES!

Wedding bells and the pitter-patter of tiny feet
can be heard in Harlequin® Romance this month
as we celebrate bouncing babies and radiant new brides!

REQUEST YOUR FREE BOOKS!
2 FREE NOVELS PLUS 2
FREE GIFTS!

HARLEQUIN *Romance*

From the Heart, For the Heart

YES! Please send me 2 FREE Harlequin® Romance novels and my 2 FREE gifts (gifts are worth about $10). After receiving them, if I don't wish to receive any more books, I can return the shipping statement marked "cancel." If I don't cancel, I will receive 6 brand-new novels every month and be billed just $3.84 per book in the U.S. or $4.24 per book in Canada. That's a savings of 15% off the cover price! It's quite a bargain! Shipping and handling is just 50¢ per book.* I understand that accepting the 2 free books and gifts places me under no obligation to buy anything. I can always return a shipment and cancel at any time. Even if I never buy another book from Harlequin, the two free books and gifts are mine to keep forever.

116/316 HDN E7T2

Name _____ (PLEASE PRINT)

Address _____ Apt. #

City _____ State/Prov. _____ Zip/Postal Code

Signature (if under 18, a parent or guardian must sign)

Mail to the **Harlequin Reader Service:**
IN U.S.A.: P.O. Box 1867, Buffalo, NY 14240-1867
IN CANADA: P.O. Box 609, Fort Erie, Ontario L2A 5X3

Not valid for current subscribers to Harlequin Romance books.

**Are you a subscriber to Harlequin Romance books
and want to receive the larger-print edition?
Call 1-800-873-8635 or visit www.ReaderService.com.**

* Terms and prices subject to change without notice. Prices do not include applicable taxes. Sales tax applicable in N.Y. Canadian residents will be charged applicable provincial taxes and GST. Offer not valid in Quebec. This offer is limited to one order per household. All orders subject to approval. Credit or debit balances in a customer's account(s) may be offset by any other outstanding balance owed by or to the customer. Please allow 4 to 6 weeks for delivery. Offer available while quantities last.

Your Privacy: Harlequin Books is committed to protecting your privacy. Our Privacy Policy is available online at www.ReaderService.com or upon request from the Reader Service. From time to time we make our lists of customers available to reputable third parties who may have a product or service of interest to you. If you would prefer we not share your name and address, please check here. ☐

Help us get it right—We strive for accurate, respectful and relevant communications. To clarify or modify your communication preferences, visit us at www.ReaderService.com/consumerchoice.

HR10R2

Harlequin Romance author Donna Alward is loved for her gorgeous rancher heroes.

Meet Wyatt as he's confronted by both a precious little pink bundle left on his doorstep and his neighbor Elli who's going to show him the ropes....

Introducing
PROUD RANCHER, PRECIOUS BUNDLE

THE SQUAWKING QUIETED as Elli picked the baby up, and Wyatt turned around, trying hard to ignore the feelings of inadequacy as Darcy immediately stopped fussing.

"Maybe she's uncomfortable. What do you think, sweetheart?" Elli turned her conversation to the baby.

"What do you think is wrong?" Wyatt asked, putting the coffee pot back on the burner.

A strange look passed over Elli's face, one that looked like guilt and panic. But it was gone quickly. "I couldn't say," she replied.

"But you were so good with her this afternoon." Wyatt put his hands on his hips.

"Lucky, that's all. I just...remembered a few things." The same strange look flitted over her features once more.

Wyatt took the coffee to the table. "You fooled me. You looked like you knew exactly what you were doing." So much so that Wyatt had felt completely inept. A feeling he despised. He was used to being the one in control.

Elli and Darcy walked the length of the kitchen and back. After a few moments, she admitted, "I haven't really cared for a baby before. The things I thought of were simply things I'd heard about. Not from experience, Mr. Black."

Her chin jutted up, closing the subject but making him

HREXP0211

want to ask the questions now pulsing through his mind. But then he remembered the old saying—*Don't look a gift horse in the mouth*. He'd benefit from whatever insight she had and be glad of it.

"I don't really know what babies need," he said. "I fed her, patted her back like you did, walked her to sleep, but every time I put her down…"

Wyatt almost groaned. Of course. He'd forgotten one important thing. He'd been so focused on getting the formula the right temperature that he'd forgotten to check her diaper. Not that he had any clue what to do there either.

Pulling calves and shoveling out stalls was far less intimidating than one tiny newborn.

"She's probably due for a diaper change, isn't she." He tried to sound nonchalant. This was a perfect opportunity. Elli must know how to change a diaper. He could simply watch her so he'd know better for the next time.

Instead, Elli came around the corner of the counter and placed Darcy back in his arms. "Here you go, Uncle Wyatt," she said lightly. "You get diaper duty. I'll fix the coffee. Cream and sugar?"

Oh boy, Wyatt thought, looking down into Darcy's pursed face, his smug plan blown to smithereens. He was in for it now.

Will sparks fly between Elli and Wyatt?

Find out in
PROUD RANCHER, PRECIOUS BUNDLE
Available February 2011 from Harlequin Romance

Try these Healthy and Delicious Spring Rolls!

INGREDIENTS

2 packages rice-paper
spring roll wrappers
(20 wrappers)

1 cup grated carrot

¼ cup bean sprouts

1 cucumber, julienned

1 red bell pepper, without
stem and seeds, julienned

4 green onions
finely chopped—
use only the green part

DIRECTIONS

1. Soak one rice-paper wrapper
   in a large bowl of hot water
   until softened.

2. Place a pinch each of carrots,
   sprouts, cucumber, bell
   pepper and green onion on the
   wrapper toward the bottom
   third of the rice paper.

3. Fold ends in and roll tightly
   to enclose filling.

4. Repeat with remaining
   wrappers. Chill before
   serving.

Find this and many more delectable recipes
including the perfect dipping sauce in